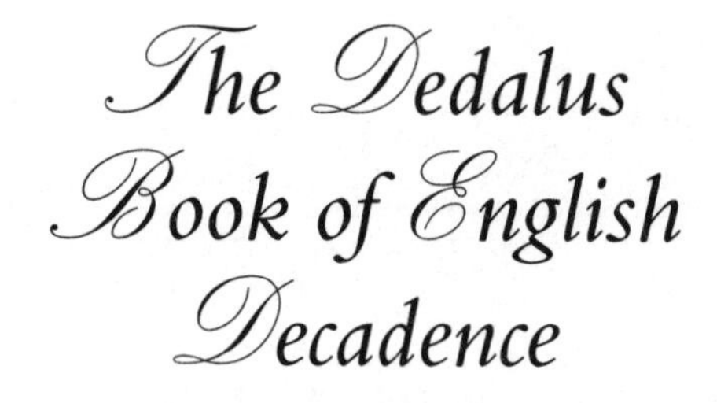

# The Dedalus Book of English Decadence

## Vile Emperors and Elegant Degenerates

James Willsher

Dedalus

Published in the UK by Dedalus Ltd, Langford Lodge,
St Judith's Lane, Sawtry, Cambs, PE28 5XE
email: DedalusLimited@compuserve.com
www: dedalusbooks.com

ISBN 1 903517 26 5

Dedalus is distributed in the United States by SCB Distributors,
15608 South New Century Drive, Gardena, California 90248
email: info@scbdistributors.com web site: www.scbdistributors.com

Dedalus is distributed in Australia & New Zealand by Peribo Pty Ltd,
58 Beaumont Road, Mount Kuring-gai N.S.W. 2080
email: peribo@bigpond.com

Dedalus is distributed in Canada by Marginal Distribution,
695, Westney Road South, Suite 14 Ajax, Ontario, L16 6M9
email: marginal@marginalbook.com web site: www.marginalbook.com

First published by Dedalus in 2004



Printed in Finland by WS Bookwell
Typeset by RefineCatch, Bungay, Suffolk



A C.I.P. listing for this book is available on request.

## THE EDITOR

The editor is a pale clerk who lives in East Anglia. He scours the country in search of lost and forgotten books.

# ACKNOWLEDGEMENTS

The editor would like to thank Eric Lane, Phil Baker and Robert Irwin for their invaluable help with compiling this book. Thanks are also due to Robert Bass, Peter Mornard, Jamie Reynolds, Dr John Byrne, Dr Paul Dawson, Professor John Woolford and Dr Malcolm Hicks.

The editor would like to thank the following for the use of copyright material:

Extracts from 'A Defence of Cosmetics' and 'Enoch Soames' by Sir Max Beerbohm are reprinted by permission of Marc Berlin.

'Ennui' by Lord Alfred Douglas is reprinted by permission of John Rubinstein and John Stratford.

'The Decadent to his Soul' by Richard Le Gallienne is reprinted by permission of the Society of Authors.

Passages from 'The Great God Pan' by Arthur Machen are reprinted by permission of A. M. Heath Author's Agents & Co. Ltd.

'In Bohemia', 'The Absinthe-Drinker', 'The Opium-Smoker', and 'Stella Maris' are reprinted by permission of Brian Read, M. A.

This is for my family and for Gulay.

# CONTENTS

# INTRODUCTION

> Ah, what a divine celebration was the *auto-da-fé* of November 1707 – how charming and modest it must have been in its holy but gay simplicity. What a fine mixture of fireworks and of flames from burning Jews, of torments below and dancing above ground, of opera . . . Ah, happy times, if only they could return . . .

This is William Beckford, millionaire aesthete, plantation owner, author of *Vathek*, and the first true English decadent. On the death of his father in 1770, the nine year old Beckford inherited one of the largest fortunes in England, derived from the spoils of empire: West Indian sugar cane. Great wealth should have brought great responsibility, but he admirably ignored this all his life, pursuing instead a career of committed sensualism. Like Byron, he courted the scandal of adulterous and incestuous affairs; like Wilde, a furious aristocrat ruined his reputation. Beckford was the godfather of an English decadence that blossomed in the 1890s, but first emerged in the latter half of the eighteenth century.

At first glance though, decadence may not appear particularly English at all. The nineteenth century looked to France for fiery poetry and prose, and with good reason. It was a time of unfettered imagination, the time of Théophile Gautier, Stéphane Mallarmé, Charles Baudelaire, Gustave Flaubert, Arthur Rimbaud, Paul Verlaine, Joris-Karl Huysmans, and Octave Mirbeau. The French decadent was typically fatigued by a world-weariness, suspicious of all passion, and had settled for a life of bored debauchery. The modern English decadent though drew deeply from the aestheticism of John Keats, the Pre-Raphaelites and Walter Pater, and so insisted upon seeing a beauty in all things, no matter how revolting. From the mid-nineteenth century it has been understood that France was the genesis of all things decadent, while Victorian England could only stand by and look on, shaking its head.

In England however, and centuries earlier, the Renaissance dramatists bequeathed a popular culture of murder and monstrosity. Christopher Marlowe's *The Tragical History of Doctor Faustus* anticipated many of the pale, young dilettantes of damnation that emerged hundreds of years later. John Webster's *The Duchess of Malfi* and Cyril Tourneur's *The Revenger's Tragedy* were unspeakably violent, but staged in a thoroughly entertaining manner. Sin was made fascinating, and depravity was disguised by great language.

Elsewhere in English history, 'Bad' King John expired from a surfeit of peaches and the composer Henry Purcell perished from alleged 'chocolate poisoning'. Both were characters clearly consumed with the sensations of the (then) exotic and rare. The Georgian society figure George Augustus Selwyn obsessively attended criminal executions, demanding the intimate details of the criminal, the crime and method of execution. He thought little of voyaging to France to indulge his morbid interests; to escape recognition on some occasions Selwyn would readily dress in women's clothing. More deviant than decadent, what all these characters have in common is that they make full use of the fruits of civilisation to indulge unwholesome appetites.

One of the earliest glimpses of English decadent writing is concerned with the extravagances of antiquity. In 1776 the first volume of Edward Gibbon's *The History of the Decline and Fall of the Roman Empire* appeared, in the same year as the American Declaration of Independence. At a point when English imperialism appeared to falter, Gibbon chose to document the collapse of empire as a concept. Things begin with Augustus halting the expansionism of Rome's ongoing conquest of the earth, a policy that allowed succeeding emperors to delegate many of their military responsibilities elsewhere. For the degenerates that followed this gave them more opportunities to indulge themselves with the fruits of the world's most flourishing economy; pursuits that quietly replaced the obligations of power. Augustus inaugurated an imperial climate much more tolerant of wayward, perverse and ultimately monstrous rulers.

Duly, a youth emerged from insurrection in Syria in A. D. 218 to become emperor of Rome, as Elagabalus, and one of history's first and most remarkable decadents. Stories abound of his depravities: he apparently smothered his guests at a dinner party to death with rose petals dropped from above; he had an artificial vagina surgically inserted; he married a (male) charioteer. Gibbon is a little more circumspect. He tells of a portrait of the new emperor arriving in Rome a while before Elagabalus's entry into the city, that horrified an already apprehensive senate. The picture showed an imperial head 'covered with a lofty tiara', with eyebrows 'tinged with black, and his cheeks painted with an artificial red and white.' What disturbed them most though was the prospect that Rome's majesty was now to be 'humbled beneath the effeminate luxury of Oriental despotism.' The dandy was born.

Gibbon attracted fierce criticism when he treated the progress of Christianity in Rome as part of the process of an empire's destruction. The account of Nero's use of the 'Galilæans' to illuminate the night is particularly barbed: for this episode he quotes Tacitus, who more or less describes the victims as vermin that deserved it, regardless of guilt. Gibbon goes on to praise the source's commitment to truth and accuracy, with only the faintest suggestion of mistaken judgment. Elsewhere he tells of the rumours of vampirism, infant sacrifice and orgiastic incest that dogged the early faithful because of their secretive worship. Worse still is the suggestion that Rome's efforts at diplomacy with the Christians were met with contempt from zealots alarmingly fond of predicting imminent apocalypse. This was too much for church-going, eighteenth-century England, but the *History* was still a great success. Incidentally, Christendom went on to retain a curious relationship with decadence. It would provide a sanctity to desecrate and the penitence with which to confess: Baudelaire, Wilde and Huysmans all died recent converts to Catholicism.

Gibbon is not a name usually associated with decadent

writers and their writing, but what he implies is that luxury corrupts, and that for any imperial society luxury is the most enduring of any achievement. Conquest of the Orient traditionally provided these luxuries (silks, gems, spices and the riches that these bring in trade): the child of empire becomes accustomed to abundance, and eventually bored by it, and then seeks more exotic matter to satisfy his curiosities. It is at this point that a decadence begins to stir. Gibbon celebrated the Orient both as one of the chief sources of Rome's wealth and of its decay.

There is a classical precedent for all degenerate conquerors of the Orient: Dionysus. The illegitimate son of Zeus was torn apart by the Titans at birth, on the instruction of a jealous Hera, wife to the king of the gods. Rescued and nurtured in a cave by nymphs, Dionysus emerged as an effeminate and foppish adult before traversing the earth with his entourage of Maenads, in order to spread the cult of the vine. Mania and monstrosity were visited upon all opposition. He subdued India, sojourned in Egypt, and then returned to Europe, before ascending to Olympus. It would be some time before myth became modern history, and other powers looked greedily eastward.

In 1704 *Arabian Nights Entertainment* appeared, translated into French by Antoine Galland and more commonly known today as *The Thousand and One Nights*. It rendered European imaginations delirious with tales of the seraglio, evil viziers and the jinnee. It was immediately translated into English and has been in print ever since. There were delicious new words to tantalise the tongue (ifrit, bazaar, harem) and new, unusual names for heroes and heroines (Ali Baba, Scheherazade, Aladdin). Fascination with all things Oriental became an ingredient in Georgian fashion: the Prince of Wales replicated Eastern architecture with his pavilion at Brighton; material swathed around the head, a *turban*, became the essential accessory for ladies of society. A publishing explosion followed, and William Jones's 1789 translation of *Sacontala*, by the Indian playwright Calidas, was to be an influence on much of the

Romantic and decadent writing of the next century. It tells of an Oriental king spellbound by the part-peasant girl, part-nymph of the title. Yearning for an immortal, impossible ideal is central to Romanticism and to decadence, prominently in John Keats' 'Endymion', and Algernon Charles Swinburne's 'Dolores'. *Sacontala* was this yearning eroticised, and after its translation it was westernised into a sensual, exotic and Oriental ideal.

All this proved irresistible to the more fevered minds of some English writers. The Eastern phantasmagoria of 'Kubla Khan' entered itself and its author, Samuel Taylor Coleridge, into the pantheon of literature; future poet laureate Robert Southey's *Thalaba the Destroyer* made his name; even Sir Walter Scott wrote *The Talisman*. What came out of all this was a generation's fascination with the Orient both as something remote and extraordinary, and yet somehow real and part of the empire. For most people, the East could only be read about in books, and mainly in translations of mythology: unsurprisingly, it was imagined as a region of magical creatures, grand palaces and the fantastical. Because of this, the exotic new beauties of the East could rather hazily merge with its exotic new horrors, such as its jinnee. The perverse appeal of the glorious and the grotesque here entered a modern, more extreme phase in England's cultural consciousness. The Orient provided a theatre for the decadent imaginations of the Occident.

William Beckford could afford not only to visit the institutions that kept Oriental texts, but also their wholesale purchase, such as Gibbon's library in Lausanne, along with artefacts, *objets d'art* and an education in Persian and Arabic. *Vathek*, his masterpiece, emerged in English in 1786, and shamelessly invested the Orient with the qualities of the gorgeous but horrid. Caliph Vathek is a prince utterly addicted to the pleasuring of the senses, but, like Beckford, he wants more, and to know more. His desire for knowledge and sensation becomes ever more insatiable: he 'thinks that he sees in whatever is past and remote from him the ideal atmosphere for the contentment of his own senses' (Praz, 1933). *Vathek* also delights with its rich language, retained in its translation from the original French by Samuel Henley. It is hypnotically alliterative, and exquisitely choice in vocabulary; 'that curious jewelled style, vivid and obscure at once, full of argot and of archaisms', as Dorian Gray might have described it. As with the Elizabethan and Jacobean dramatists, pleasures are to be had from horrors in great costumes of language. Beckford wrote his decadent appetites into the monstrous *Vathek*, whose unhealthy pursuits do not provide a blueprint for the decadent lifestyle, like Huysmans' *À Rebours* ('Against Nature'), but instead a cautionary tale in the manner of Marlowe's *The Tragical History of Doctor Faustus*, or Wilde's *The Picture of Dorian Gray*. Beckford's Orient is both an exquisite and hideous experience.

*Sacontala* acclimatised Georgian literary tastes to an eroticised Orient; the emerging English decadence adulterated it into something much more unsavoury. The marriage of beauty and terror was initially Orientalised, as in *Vathek*: 'Kubla Khan' has its 'woman wailing for her demon-lover'; Thomas De Quincey confesses that, whilst in opiate reverie, he found himself 'kissed, with cancerous kisses, by crocodiles'. On the Continent *femmes fatale* moved eastward: Théophile Gautier produced *Une Nuit de Cléopâtre* after *Mademoiselle De Maupin*; Gustave Flaubert followed *Madame Bovary* with *Salammbô*. Charles Baudelaire translated his lust for his 'Black Venus' Jeanne Duval into any number of poems ('Le Vampire', 'Duellum', 'Les Bijoux' . . .). By the end of the century and back in England, the affair became fatal and all the more seductive for it: witness Wilde's 'Charmides' and *Salomé*.

With regard to Coleridge and De Quincey, it is interesting to see how readily images of the East were appropriated by the ecstasies and desolations of opium. This is a drug that is horrifyingly appropriate for a philosophy that marries the painful and the pleasurable. Opium regularly appears in the stories of Edgar Allan Poe, and in 'Ligeia' its association with the East is clear: 'Wild visions, opium-engendered, flitted, shadow-like, before me. I gazed with unquiet eye upon the sarcophagi . . .'

The peeled nerves of some of Coleridge's poems and the horrors of his addiction (see 'The Pains of Sleep' and 'A Fragment' that precedes 'Kubla Khan') are unmistakably decadent. He was an ill man in every respect, and when you consider the extraordinary writing he was producing at the time, this illness can seem no longer tragic, but horribly *interesting*. A robust, healthy condition produces robust, healthy thought and writing; this holds no interest for the decadent, who prefers a languid or unhinged state of mind. Why? Because delirium and shattered nerves offer new, unfamiliar sensations and ways of looking at the world. Georgian poets William Cowper and Christopher Smart both suffered from lengthy periods of insanity, but kept on writing throughout. Smart underwent years of incarceration in an asylum, and, like Coleridge, only found a degree of peace in Christianity. This is from 'Jubilate Agno':

> For I bless God the Postmaster general & all
> conveyancers of letters under his care especially Allen &
> Shelvock.
> For my grounds in Canaan shall infinitely compensate
> for the flats & maynes of Staindrop Moor.
> For the praise of God can give to a mute fish the notes of
> a nightingale.

This is the kind of distorted view of things that appeals to the decadent; unsurprisingly, some of Smart's best works such as 'A Song To David' were not included in a 1791 collection, as deemed 'not acceptable to the reader' by editors. However unsettling this concept may be, the insane see things *differently*. Narcotics offered a fleeting glimpse of this. Opium, alcohol and laudanum (opium dissolved in alcohol) were the drugs of choice for many of the nineteenth-century's writers. Oscar Wilde tried hashish in Egypt and favoured imported, opium-tinged Egyptian cigarettes back in London; Ernest Dowson experimented with hashish at university before alcoholic melancholy consumed him as an adult.

It is too easy an explanation, however, to say that the

decadent demands to be anaesthetised from the everyday business of existence. Much of the writing produced after these experiences makes for unsettling reading, and cannot have been inspired by a blissful, mindless hour. No, the decadent seeks both paradise *and* horror in his pursuit of new, exotic sensations. The great Charles Baudelaire, avatar of the French decadence and seemingly read by anyone of note in the latter half of the nineteenth-century, would deferentially refer to and re-work passages from De Quincey's *Confessions of an English Opium-Eater* in 'On Wine and Hashish' (1851) and 'The Poem of Hashish' (1860). By unhappy accident, Coleridge and De Quincey established the model for generations to come of the young and intoxicated.

Georgian decadence concerned itself with arabesques of east and west, beauty and horror, eroticism and death. This proved dangerous. In the age of Romanticism the poet exalted himself as a martyr for his art: suddenly in England there was remarkable writing being brandished by equally remarkable characters. The writer was not only recognisable in his work, but was realised by it. The image of a pale and interesting young thing furiously at work upon a masterpiece was born in this time. In the Age of Revolution, as Thomas Paine named the latter half of the eighteenth century, absolute commitment to the cause, whatever the cause was, became compulsory.

Ideas of freedom formed in this era laid the foundation for all future decadent behaviour. The American and French Revolutions had been sparked from new ideas of liberty which resounded through the whole imperial world. First it was social, economic, and political thought that came under fire, and then it was the turn of religious, sexual and moral principles. William Godwin's *Enquiry Concerning Political Justice* and Thomas Paine's *Rights of Man* and *The Age of Reason* were the key texts of the new forum on freedoms in England. With incredible irony, the Romantic generation that revolted *against* the decadence of their empire, which was founded on plutocratic democracy and slavery, managed to engineer the intellectual architecture for the decadence of the self.

This was achieved through decades of steady collapse in all forms of belief, before metamorphosing into a form of aestheticised nihilism. The Age of Revolution did not mark the end of the Age of Empire, however. Not all governments collapsed overnight, and neither were the new, liberal politics properly implemented, as witnessed by Napoleonic France's descent into dictatorship. By the end of the century all Paine, Godwin and Bonaparte had achieved was the hollowing out of belief in anything, old or new. Any *fin de siècle* society experiences a nervous uncertainty of progress, celebration and apocalypse, the mood which gave rise to the great flowering of English decadence in the 1890s. So it is unsurprising that the closing decades of the eighteenth century resounded with the explosion of the Gothic novel. The ruins of castles, religions and innocence that feature in the writing of Horace Walpole, Ann Radcliffe and Matthew Lewis demonstrate the sense of living in a world falling down. When faith in the good of all things flounders, the individual looks elsewhere, anywhere, to pleasure, to oblivion; a decadence beckons.

Edgar Allan Poe wrote on this many decades later, in 'The Imp of the Perverse'. His claim is that any desire for good needs to be 'excited' by knowing why not to do evil, from knowledge usually provided by law or religion. The 'excitement' may prove too much of course, and then 'through its promptings we act, for the reason that we should *not* . . . to do wrong for the wrong's sake'. The decadent creed.

William Beckford appears from his life and letters as a man recklessly trying to live the life of his own doomed Caliph Vathek. His dangerous charisma and capricious passions for adultery proved horribly infectious to those around him, often resulting in scandal that they could not afford. This is from the correspondence of Louisa Beckford, wife of his cousin Peter, and a disregarded lover: 'William, my lovely infernal! how gloriously you write of iniquities . . . like another Lucifer you would tempt Angels to forsake their coelestial abode, and sink with you into the black infernal gulph.' At times Beckford seems the parody of the pale and distempered decadent, luxuriating in ill-health: 'This morning I feel a universal malaise', 'My languor is such that I can write no more', 'I am still very languid.' One episode in his life, however, proves him beyond doubt the godfather of all English decadence. At Christmas in 1781 Beckford and some companions, including a theatre pyrotechnician famed for his 'necromantic' lighting and effects, abandoned themselves to the vaulted intricacies of his family home's halls and corridors. These had been transformed into a form of subterranean boudoir by 'the vapour of wood aloes ascending in wreaths from cassolettes placed low on the silken carpets in porcelain salvers of the richest japan.' Forty years later Beckford still talked in his letters of the, 'delirium of delight into which our young and fervid bosoms were cast,' by this, 'Demon Temple deep beneath the earth set apart for tremendous mysteries'. This anticipated the *fictional* experiments in sensory disorder of Huysmans' Des Esseintes by an entire century.

The damned of the underworld lend their stories to the three *Episodes of Vathek*, which were written as a continuation of *Vathek*. They were published only in 1912, as Beckford lost heart after initial fury at their removal from the unsanctioned, anonymous 1786 publication of his masterpiece. The *Episodes* gleefully parade incest, necrophilia, heresy, fratricide and despotism against a sumptuously Oriental backdrop. His letters refer to the fourth, unpublished, and perhaps unpublishable tale of 'Motassem', which he fears as too much for his readers, with extremities beyond extremities of, 'the grandiose, the graceful, the whorish and the holy'. Beckford's stories and debaucheries mark the origin of the decadent appetite for damnation, which came to a head a hundred years later in Oscar Wilde's very willing fall from disgrace into utter destruction.

Caliph Vathek's ferocious and dangerous pursuit of sensation anticipated entire generations of impressionable youth. These are the casualties of the age of Romanticism: Percy Bysshe Shelley drowned at thirty; Lord Byron was bled to death by his doctors in revolutionary Greece, at thirty-six; John Keats dead from consumption, at twenty-six. William

Wordsworth lived on to become a respectable establishment poet: Shelley felt grief enough to address this lamentable failure to expire in verse ('To Wordsworth'). Coleridge's post-1800 poetry rarely lived up to his astonishing potential, after decades of drug addiction and Christianity. Decadents and Romantics alike were finished by ideas: Byron's pursuit of doom and glory funded Greek resistance against Turkish rule; he died never having seen combat. Shelley put his fate into the hands of the elements, and perished in a storm.

The 1890s saw the most degenerate descendants of the Georgian era attract the name of, 'The Tragic Generation', a phrase coined by W. B. Yeats. Although due in the main to tuberculosis, this was exacerbated by riotously intemperate lifestyles. These are the victims of those years: Lionel Johnson dead at thirty-five, alcoholic and insomniac; Ernest Dowson cut down at thirty-three from T. B.; Oscar Wilde deceased at forty-six.

Byron in particular idolised Beckford, claiming *Vathek* as his personal Bible; the exotic ferocity of his own Eastern tales such as *The Corsair* and *The Giaour* only intensified the Georgian appetite for things Oriental. Byron is the most recognisable influence on the lifestyles of the 1890s. He made little distinction between his writing and himself, and insisted on taking nothing seriously. Why? Because behind a mask of insouciance, you can *almost* get away with . . . anything. Sensation was the force that extorted from him his relentless pursuit of new experience. Like Beckford, he was the quintessential child of empire, proudly aristocratic, and whose instantly gratified appetites became ever more perverse, particularly while on the Continent. In a letter he admits, 'excessive susceptibility to immediate impressions'; the hero of *Childe Harold* claims addiction to, 'revel and ungodly glee.'

Byron came of age in the era of Napoleon's dictatorship, which was the final failure of belief in the Age of Revolution. Idealism had never surfaced in his writing before, and after this it never could. Everywhere he looked he saw boredom and disaster, and escape from this became his end in life, like a thorough decadent. 'The great object of life is sensation – to feel that we exist – even in pain,' he wrote in a letter: existence for him was a cultivated addiction to forbidden sensations, and eventually those of destruction. This is the core of *Manfred* and *Cain; Don Juan* celebrates an unending parade of experiences. The poet needed, 'the feeling of fatality in order to appreciate the flow of life . . . like Satan, Byron wished to experience the feeling of being struck with full force by the vengeance of Heaven.' (Praz, 1933) This was to be got by ultimate, 'ambrosial' sin. He was attracted to Augusta Leigh because of her startling resemblance to him; that she was his half-sister must have made her absolutely irresistible.

Others wrote the concerns of the times into a form of horticultural lyricism. John Keats suffused his verse with a voluptuousness which anticipated the perfume and luxury of the Pre-Raphaelite and decadent modes. Such a rich, narcotic style provided the decadent reader with a heady lexicon for studies in the exquisite, and latterly for prettifying the grotesque. With Keats the necessity for elegance in all things was established. His words intoxicate, most notably in the Odes, and the luscious paganisms of 'Endymion' and the 'Hyperion' fragments provided a model for Swinburne, Dante Gabriel Rossetti and the writers of the 1890s. Incidentally, veneration for the great texts of antiquity led some writers to Neoplatonism, and then onto their own ornate forms of paganism: Shelley, George Moore and Wilde. This abandonment of Christianity horrified others, however. Keats' recital of 'Hymn to Pan' from *Endymion* elicited disgust from Wordsworth at, 'The Immortal Dinner' of 28 December, 1817. Keats inaugurated a new era of writing, and in a letter to his friend Richard Woodhouse he revealed his rather modern conceptions of the poetical faculty:

> it is not itself – it has no self – it is every thing and nothing – It has no character – it enjoys light and shade; it lives in gusto, be it foul or fair, high or low, rich or poor, mean or elevated – It has as much delight in conceiving an Iago as an Imogen. What shocks the virtuous philosop[h]er, delights the camelion poet. It does no

harm from its relish of the dark side of things any more than from its taste for the bright one; because they both end in speculation.

Effacement of self amidst sensation? Beauty in the 'dark side of things'? Moral concerns eschewed for 'speculation'? Keats had almost written a proto-decadent philosophy, and for this the writers of the *fin de siècle* regarded him with the greatest esteem. A July day in 1894 was to mark the unveiling of a new bust of Keats in Hampstead Church. For this ostensibly unremarkable occasion the congregation was unexpectedly swelled by what seemed the entire cultural firmament of the time. All literary London attended, including an evidently tubercular Aubrey Beardsley, who was observed stumbling about the graveyard.

The world was changing, though. While King George IV indulged himself in the 1820s, pressure for reform intensified, particularly of antiquated criminal and industrial legislation. From this came the 1832 Reform Bill and the 1833 Factory Act. Two years later, in France, Théophile Gautier gave the world the charming abnormalities of *Mademoiselle De Maupin*. In 1837 Victoria became Queen, and England entered a new phase of engineering and industrial achievement. With Albert and her children the Queen was mother to both a family and to a nation; the air of domesticity was palpable in the title of Charles Dickens's periodical *Household Words*, which he edited from 1850. In France at this time Gustave Flaubert was prosecuted for the amorality of *Madame Bovary*, and in 1857 Charles Baudelaire made the unsavoury wonderfully interesting with *Les Fleurs du Mal*. After Napoleon's fall in 1815, France suffered over fifty years of constitutional muddle in the form of alternating republics and emperors, whilst England subdued the earth with war and commerce. As the star of the French decadence was boldly in the ascendant, any glimmerings in England were extinguished by the spirit of progress and reform. This explosion of French imagination seemed to follow on from the nihilist sensualism of Byron, a bestseller on the Continent as in England. The appeals to sense and feeling of John Keats would go on to shape English decadence, soon to re-emerge in the form of a new aestheticism. Fascination with the Orient had repackaged the idea of beauty and horror from the Renaissance plays, and art never fully recovered.

It is Oxford, and not London, that can claim the great genesis of the modern English decadence. John Ruskin graduated from the university and started writing the first volume of *Modern Painters*, which was published in 1843: his insistence upon the potency of imagination sculpted the culture of aestheticism that followed. Matthew Arnold, Professor of Poetry at Oxford from 1857, in *The Function of Criticism at the Present Time* campaigned for a new 'disinterestedness' in modern thought. This was born from his vitriolic views on middle-class prudery, and the eminently Victorian, 'practical view of things'. This disinterestedness should disregard the popular, pragmatic opinion of a matter, and instead unfetter the imagination, allowing, 'free play of the mind on all subjects which it touches.' Impressionism was born, and in England. It is worth noting that Arnold's profession for thirty-five years was as an inspector of schools, which he held whilst conceiving and writing these ideas.

In 1866 English decadence found its *enfant terrible*. Algernon Charles Swinburne's *Poems and Ballads* appeared with the author boldly proclaiming his work 'the final achievement' of all verse. He had received his education at Oxford at the time of Arnold. With 'Faustine' and 'Anactoria' depravity and ecstasy were wedded in what must have seemed some of the most unrepentantly unsafe writing ever conceived. In consummately measured metre and with the articulacy of a confirmed lexical gourmet, it was the extravagant use of language that provoked the controversy. Monstrous lusts are ornately reimagined with words, and appear much less distasteful for it; appealing, even. Pagan Swinburne had horrified church-going, Victorian England, just as he had set out to do. *Poems and Ballads* was immediately reprinted, and the nation's youth chanted these lines in its streets:

Thou hast conquered, O pale Galilean; the world has
grown grey from thy breath;

Swinburne nearly succeeded in living an existence as extraordinary as his verse. Guy de Maupassant recalls a luncheon at the Englishman's residence at Étretat in 1874, where the host offered no wine, but only spirits, and allowed a large monkey to gambol inside the little cottage. Portfolios of full-length male nudes were paraded after dining. Maupassant noticed how much Swinburne trembled, and five years later his dissipations had duly ruined him enough to necessitate a removal to Putney, where he lived settled and sobered, tended by his friend Theodore Watts-Dunton, until his death in 1909.

Five years after the furore of *Poems and Ballads*, and one year after Dante Gabriel Rossetti's collected verse, some had simply had enough. Robert Buchanan's essay, 'The Fleshly School of Poetry' appeared pseudonymously in volume 18, August-November 1871, of the *Contemporary Review*. It was intended as a righteously scathing attack upon the preponderance of 'inappropriate' themes in modern English verse. Rossetti suffered the bulk of Buchanan's indignation, singled out for daring to include in both his poems and paintings:

> the same combination of the simple and the grotesque, the same morbid deviation from healthy forms of life, the same sense of weary, wasting, yet exquisite sensuality; nothing virile, nothing tender, nothing completely sane; a superfluity of extreme sensibility, of delight in beautiful forms, hues, tints, and a deep-seated indifference to all agitating forces and agencies, all tumultuous griefs and sorrows, all the thunderous stress of life, and all the straining storm of speculation.

Apparently, it was, 'neither poetic, nor manly, nor even human,' to make these things the themes of whole poems: it was 'simply nasty.' Buchanan perfectly encapsulated the opinions of the practical Victorian middle-class householder, of the sort that Matthew Arnold manifestly despised. No 'free play of the mind' was permitted: what the Victorians asked of art was to be of sound moral standing in form and matter, nothing more, and nothing less. For the modern-day reader, however, Buchanan inevitably provides some unintentionally amusing material. Sermonizing against the brazenly 'fleshly' verses of Rossetti's 'Love-Lily', he claims that, 'to many people who live in the country they may even appear beautiful'; later on he laments the poetical fate of, 'young gentlemen with animal faculties morbidly developed by too much tobacco and too little exercise.'

These last words condemn the *ennui* and *impuissance*, or the world-weariness and sense of powerlessness, of decadent youth amidst the relentless achievement of empire. England was now 'the workshop of the world', its distances criss-crossed with canals and railways. Global trade flourished: in 1839 British merchants objected to the Chinese authorities' seizure of their smuggled opium, and instigated the Opium War, which China lost in 1842, ceding Hong Kong. By the late nineteenth-century the empire had also waged war against Afghanistan, Burma, Kashmir, Nepal, and the Punjab, and had crushed the Sepoy Rebellion, sparked by ethnic intolerance. Languor has little to do with *progress*.

In 1873 the liturgy of the aesthetical sensualists arrived, from the pen of a reticent Fellow of Brasenose College in Oxford. Walter Pater's *Studies in the History of the Renaissance* disregarded any documentary premise in its title, opting instead for impressionistic sallies into deliberate factual misrepresentation and vagueness. Truth dissipates into a fog of contemplation, as Pater's subjects, notably the Mona Lisa, are only faintly discernible from the intoxicated criticism that they elicit. The Romantic spirit of absolute commitment to art and ideals started to dissolve under this new mode of abstract writing. From these hothouse pages the great English decadence blossomed forth, and to this day the conclusion remains a danger to its reader. The hedonism provoked by those closing comments absolutely appalled Pater, however, to the extent of their removal from the book's second edition. The writer was concerned that his conclusion, 'might possibly mislead some of those young men into whose hands it might fall.' One of those impressionable youths was to be Oscar Wilde, who appropriated his pleasingly ambiguous relationship to sincerity from this book.

By the 1880s art was the glass through which to view the decadent world. After Keats' and Pater's heady aestheticism all sensation, 'foul' or 'fair', was to be weighed for its exquisiteness. An encounter with the profane could be just as pleasing as a sense of guiltless propriety. This is what leads the decadent into dimly-lit docklands and opium dens in the small hours of the morning.

By the closing decades of the century imperial grandeur had reached its apogee: in 1877 Victoria had been proclaimed empress of India. Wilde, in 'Theoretikos' from *Poems* (1881), disdains the age as some, 'vile traffic-house,' where, 'rude people rage with ignorant cries / Against an heritage of centuries.' Rather, 'in dreams of Art / And loftiest culture I would stand apart'. The decadent now proclaims his renunciation of the dire world's affairs. In London, on the 20th of February, 1885, James McNeill Whistler delivered his 'Ten O'Clock' lecture, which savagely satirised this current of things. With tongue-in-cheek, Whistler spoke of an antiquity when, 'people lived in marvels of art,' and went about their daily business in a state of uninterrupted artistic reverie. He wasn't the only one scoffing: Gilbert and Sullivan's *Patience* mocks these high-minded affectations with the caricature of Reginald Bunthorne.

So the decadent intoxicated his vision of the world by means of art and sensation, at the expense of society, and then morality. George Moore in his 1888 *Confessions of a Young Man* is utterly disgusted that his enjoyment of the pyramids at Giza must be tempered in some way, by consideration of the slavery and cruelty involved in their construction. How did the discussions in Plato's *Symposium* on the benefits of great and beautiful things come to this? These are the aesthetics of the perverse. The English now had more opportunities to indulge themselves with the fruits of the world's most flourishing economy, pursuits that quietly replaced the obligations of power.

It is the dawning of the *fin de siècle* in London, closing the century that had made England the imperial and commercial capital of the world. It is difficult to exaggerate the importance of London for the erupting decadence: the 1890s even saw a sub-genre of verse emerge in the form of ecstatic paeans to the capital, a rousing example being Richard Le Gallienne's, 'A Ballad of London'. Quite simply, the city offered the young man of appetite anything and everything: pleasure and pain, the sumptuous and the squalid. Imperial civilisation was producing marvels such as the telephone and the fountain pen, and in London the excitement of all this modernity was married with the splendour of its history, visible from the skyline of Westminster down to the biography of any street corner. The capital was an intoxicating playground, capable of merging any extremity: ancient and modern, familiar and exotic, foul and fair.

However, another emperor would be proclaimed on June the 20th, 1890, when Lippincott's Magazine first published *The Picture of Dorian Gray*. Wilde wrote little else of such stridently decadent calibre, other than *Salomé* (1893 in French, 1894 in English), and its book form, available by April of the succeeding year, remains the most famous of all English decadent works. It is the life and death of the nineteenth-century English decadent; or, the modern *Vathek*. Where his poems demonstrate an affection for Baudelaire and Swinburne with their marriage of classical allusions and ornate profanities, the novel acknowledges the influence of Joris-Karl Huysmans' anti-hero Des Esseintes, in Dorian's forays into obscure realms of knowledge and sensation. However, the dialogues, the luxurious language and the moral fable are pure Wilde, and entirely the product of his adopted, imperial island.

There had been a coterie of young disciples around Wilde since the 1880s listening to his wit and words, and with their avatar's success they began to assume an importance of their own as the writers and characters of the decadent nineties. Richard Le Gallienne witnessed one of Wilde's lectures in Birkenhead in 1883, and went on to become a poet, writer and friend. Max Beerbohm had been introduced to him in

1888, and became an instant convert. As quick and sharp with words as his mentor was languid and delightful, Beerbohm was to be the Puck of the age, pricking the balloons of those who took things a little too seriously, with his caricatures and satirical works like *The Happy Hypocrite* and *Enoch Soames*. Wilde met John Gray in 1889, and this, 'youth in the Temple,' had fascinated him enough for him to appropriate the young man's surname. Aubrey Beardsley had first been encountered after appearing at Edward Burne-Jones's house in 1891, to show the older artist his work. Oscar, staying at the time, was immediately impressed and took a keen interest in the young man, engaging him to provide the illustrations for *Salomé*, some of Beardsley's greatest work. Wilde claimed later to have invented him.

The author of *Dorian Gray* was not the only bright force of the decadent nineties. Between 1890 and 1891 Ernest Rhys and and a young William Butler Yeats convened The Rhymers' Club, which would meet at the Cheshire Cheese in Fleet Street, an establishment which still exists today. Members included John Davidson, Ernest Dowson, G. A. Greene, Lionel Johnson, Richard Le Gallienne, Victor Plarr, Ernest Radford and Arthur Symons. A disparate lot, they all shared, 'uncritical admiration,' of Pater, whose achievements with imaginative truth were felt to have dissipated the need for absolute commitment to anything. The literary languor extended to exclude the uncouth indecencies of French decadence. They all read Baudelaire and Verlaine, but the English decadent of the 1890s sinned with subtlety, and took some care to guard himself; Wilde's wit averted disaster, but only for a while. John Davidson branded the Rhymers as lacking in, 'blood and guts,' for this mindfulness, according to Yeats's *Autobiographies*. Symons, the most vocal devotee, published an essay in *Harper's New Monthly Magazine* in November, 1893, entitled, 'The Decadent Movement in Literature'. It proclaimed the new art wonderfully reminiscent of the Latin decadence (the prime exponent being Petronius, with his rampant *Satyricon*); its two main branches of expression being the Symbolist and Impressionist modes, and with an insistence upon the 'truth' *and* 'perversity' of its subject matter. Symons's own poems are unashamedly concerned with exotic theatres, sordid liaisons and squalor, and are satisfyingly frank amidst other Rhymers's studied insouciance.

The *fin de siècle* enjoyed its own publishing frenzies. John Lane and Elkin Mathews of The Bodley Head publishers took full advantage of an opening in the market for the sensational. *The Yellow Book* quarterly was conceived in the cafés of Dieppe in 1893, where bohemian London was sojourning. With Henry Harland as editor and Aubrey Beardsley in charge of the artwork, it appeared on the 16th of April, 1894. Yellow was a rather provocative choice, as lewd French publications of the time were conspicuously yellow-backed. A contributor describes the sheer presence the quarterly had:

> The [shop] window seemed to be gibbering, our eyes to be filled with incurable jaundice . . . And the inside of the book! It is full of cleverness as one expects to find in those who dwell below light and hope and love and aspiration.

This was from Michael Field (the pseudonym of Katharine Bradley and Edith Cooper); material was provided by Max Beerbohm, Richard Garnett, George Gissing, the Rhymers, Fr. Rolfe / 'Baron Corvo', and Theodore Wratislaw, amongst others. The first issue included Symons's 'Stella Maris', which concerned an encounter with a prostitute, and only added to the anticipated *succès de scandale*. The *Westminster Gazette* indignantly demanded an, 'Act of Parliament to make this sort of thing illegal'; *Punch* declared that, 'uncleanliness is next to Bodliness.' Henry James, a somewhat surprising contributor, claimed to, 'hate too much the horrid aspect and company of the whole publication'; despite this he continued to submit material.

London awoke one morning to this headline, however: 'Arrest of Oscar Wilde, *Yellow Book* under his arm.' Biographical myth claims he was actually holding *Aphrodite* by Pierre Louÿs, a French, yellow-bound publication, but this had yet to be published. Whatever the truth, the headline was enough: the periodical's Vigo Street offices were set upon by a mob, and the taint of acquaintance ensured Beardsley's dismissal. E. F. Benson claimed that after this *The Yellow Book*, 'turned grey overnight', although it continued for another nine volumes that included material from John Buchan, H. G. Wells and Arnold Bennett. Great Victorian writing, but not decadent.

Symons refused to let the idea of a flagship for English decadence die however, and established *The Savoy* with the publisher of erotica (and notorious debauchee) Leonard Smithers. Symons was the editor, who then brought in Beardsley. The cover for the first issue originally depicted one of the illustrator's small, bizarre creatures urinating on a copy of *The Yellow Book*, but this was prudently removed by Smithers. Though it attracted contributions from literary heavyweights such as Joseph Conrad, George Bernard Shaw, and W. B. Yeats *The Savoy* appeared in January 1896 and folded in the December of that year. W. H. Smith's booksellers refused to stock it, in objection to one of Yeats's illustrations; this ruined sales. Wilde's debacle had infected English decadence with something slow and incurable.

Two careers illustrate the curious creature of 1890s decadence best. Ernest Dowson wrote melancholy into musical verse, with perfect, simple grace. 'Cynara' and 'They Are Not Long' are the most celebrated of his works, which introduced the phrases, 'gone with the wind' and, 'the days of wine and roses'. With his words the horrors of decadence are far off in the soft distance. Dowson the man though was a complete catastrophe, even by the French standard of Paul Verlaine. He staggered through the nineties in an absinthe haze: a day at his father's chronically failing dockyard; a night of drunkenness; and a few hours drowsing on a friend's chair before beginning again. The impossible love in his poems was for the twelve-year-old daughter of a restaurant owner, who came of age and married someone else. He never made any money, and he died claiming a life of letters wasn't working for him. No affectation, no studied languor, Ernest Dowson lived and died an English decadent.

Aubrey Beardsley contracted tuberculosis when he was seven. In his teens he illustrated in his spare time, at twenty-one he produced masterpieces. Symons described this industriousness as, 'the fatal speed of those who are to die young.' Beardsley's drawings are painstakingly accomplished and peculiar, and utterly appropriate to the time. He illustrated the age of decadence, and was the toast of decadent London: *Salomé, The Yellow Book, The Savoy, Plays* by John Davidson, *The Great God Pan* by Arthur Machen, *The Houses of Sin* by Vincent O'Sullivan, *Verses* by Ernest Dowson: all decorated by him. Beardsley's was the style of English decadence, but the one thing he utterly despised was the substance of the decadent. Amidst dandies, he dressed always as for the office. Whilst working with him, he resented Wilde's avuncular quips, and was horrified to find himself associated with the writer's homosexual clique. Beardsley accepted John Lane's invitation to work on *The Yellow Book* only on the condition that Wilde was prohibited from contributing; he later referred to Lane's The Bodley Head publishers as, 'The Sodley Bed'. The consumptive also loathed Dowson, probably for his reckless living. The brief association with Leonard Smithers and his dissolute lifestyle quickly brought on his end. Aubrey Beardsley produced a life's work in just a few fierce years. His *œuvre* is the most astonishing of the period, yet his interest in the mode remained almost exclusively professional.

The full force of decadence was proving unsustainable, and was eating itself from the inside. Wilde's disaster notwithstanding, by the mid-1890s the pose of insouciance had diseased English decadence irreparably. A structure that toyed with its own sincerity had been built upon the sandy foundations of Impressionism. Napoleon had shipwrecked idealism at the birth of the century, and by its close Nietzsche's, 'Death of God' concept did more of the same. Darwin's, *Origin of Species* (1859) and, *The Descent of Man* (1871), replaced conviction with ideas, and along with Pater this atmosphere of uncertainty perfected English decadence: commit to nothing, as it's all momentary anyway. The brilliance of the sensation was that it never pretended to be anything other than fleeting; the hideous irony being that the habitual sensualist eventually craved it otherwise. The writers of the last decade of the nineteenth century suffered commitment to a cause that denied any commitment. Symons was ingeniously polite about this:

> London is not the atmosphere of movements or of societies . . . In England art has to be protected not only against the world, but against one's self and one's fellow artist, by a kind of affected modesty which is the Englishman's natural pose, half pride and half self-distrust.

There was nothing left to do but enjoy the posture, for as long as it lasted. After Wilde, that wasn't long at all.

This was not the end of all baroque abomination, though. The 1880s short story phenomenon of Sir Arthur Conan Doyle paved the way for some gruesome things to come. Outside the poetical circles of the Rhymers and Wilde, others had luridly reimagined the short story and novella forms. Arthur Machen used to drink with Ernest Dowson, and his writing is similarly understated; stories such as, 'The Inmost Light', are all the more disturbing for this, even by today's standards of sophistication. R. Murray Gilchrist wrote ornate, supernatural fictions of an odd, demoniac beauty, before moving on to realism in the twentieth century. Count Stanislaus Eric Stenbock clearly enjoyed the 1890s as a flamboyant *bon viveur* and literary dilettante in homoerotic horror; he outlived his prose collection, *Studies of Death* (1894), by just a year before his excesses with alcohol and narcotics killed him. Writers like these absorbed the ether of decadence around at the time, and greatly enriched the horror genre.

The new century demanded realism and modernism, and an end to ornate froth. The self would speak in monologue with stark frankness of the world's dour and terrible concerns.

But this new language of isolation had already been written some years before, by decadents fatigued by the details of existence. H. B. Marriott Watson's, 'The Dead Wall', appeared in *The Yellow Book*, marking another mutation of style into what would become the existentialist novel and the novel of introspective obsession: W. Somerset Maugham's, *Of Human Bondage*, could not have been written without the achievements of the decadent writers.

The celebrated decadence of the *fin de siècle* certainly burned a while with its, 'hard, gem-like flame' as Pater had wished, before the law of the Victorians stamped it out. It enjoyed a curious intimacy with nineteenth-century empire: the French decadence emerged in times of unrest and uncertainty; the English at the peak of imperial power. Degeneration simply proved a form of progress like any other. At the end, it was either death or confession: Wilde, Gray and Beardsley all embraced Catholicism after the searing heat of decadence; perhaps guilt, paradise and eternal torment were the only things left that still appealed.

A final portrait of the decadent:

> He avidly loves strange loves and, fierce with beauty, he plucks strange flowers.

And of decadence:

> Here are apples of Sodom, here are the very hearts of vices, and tender sins.

These lines are from, 'In Honour of Dorian and His Creator', which John Davidson wrote originally in Latin; they make a fitting epitaph. All ideals collapse, and even nihilism ends devouring itself. Decadence is the only mode which recognises this and gets on with things, namely a soft oblivion. The rise and fall of Oscar Wilde marks the final, greatest flowering of the English decadence before that hell-on-earth: the Great

War. This was the apocalypse of all imperial idiocy, when vile emperors really did fiddle while the world burned.

> So now all things are damn'd one feels at ease.
> – Lord Byron, Canto the Sixth, xxiii, of *Don Juan*.

1

## TAEDIUM VITAE

*Oscar Wilde*

To stab my youth with desperate knives, to wear
This paltry age's gaudy livery,
To let each base hand filch my treasury,
To mesh my soul within a woman's hair,
And to be Fortune's lackeyed groom, – I swear
I love it not! These things are less to me
Than the thin foam that frets upon the sea,
Less than the thistledown of summer air
Which hath no seed: better to stand aloof
Far from these slanderous fools who mock my life
Knowing me not, better the lowliest roof
Fit for the meanest hind to sojourn in,
Than to go back to that hoarse cave of strife
Where my white soul first kissed the mouth of sin.

## 2

## Passages from
## THE HISTORY OF THE DECLINE AND FALL OF THE ROMAN EMPIRE
### *Edward Gibbon*

from Chapter VI

A rational voluptuary adheres with invariable respect to the temperate dictates of nature, and improves the gratifications of sense by social intercourse, endearing connections, and the soft colouring of taste and the imagination. But Elagabalus (I speak of the emperor of that name), corrupted by his youth, his country, and his fortune, abandoned himself to the grossest pleasures with ungoverned fury, and soon found disgust and satiety in the midst of his enjoyments. The inflammatory powers of art were summoned to his aid: the confused multitude of women, of wines, and of dishes, and the studied variety of attitudes and sauces, served to revive his languid appetites. New terms and new inventions in these sciences, the only ones cultivated and patronised by the monarch, signalized his reign, and transmitted his infamy to succeeding times. A capricious prodigality supplied the want of taste and elegance; and whilst Elagabalus lavished away the treasures of his people in the wildest extravagance, his own voice and that of his flatterers applauded a spirit and magnificence unknown to the tameness of his predecessors. To confound the order of seasons and climates, to sport with the passions and the prejudices of his subjects, and to subvert every law of nature and decency, were in the number of his most delicious amusements. A long train of concubines, and a rapid succession of wives, among whom was a vestal virgin, ravished by force from her sacred asylum, were insufficient to satisfy the impotence of his passions. The master of the Roman world affected to copy the dress and manners of the female sex, preferred the distaff to the sceptre, and dishonoured the dignities of the empire by distributing them among his numerous lovers; one of whom was publicly invested with the title and authority of the emperor's, or, as he more properly styled himself, of the empress's husband.

It may seem probable, the vices and follies of Elagabalus have been adorned by fancy, and blackened by prejudice. Yet confining ourselves to the public scenes displayed before the Roman people, and attested by grave and contemporary historians, their inexpressible infamy surpasses that of any other age or country. The licence of an eastern monarch is secluded from the eye of curiosity by the inaccessible walls of his seraglio. The sentiments of honour and gallantry have introduced a refinement of pleasure, a regard for decency, and a respect for the public opinion, into the modern courts of Europe; but the corrupt and opulent nobles of Rome gratified every vice that could be collected from the mighty conflux of nations and manners. Secure of impunity, careless of censure, they lived without restraint in the patient and humble society of their slaves and parasites. The emperor, in his turn, viewing every rank of his subjects with the same contemptuous indifference, asserted without control his sovereign privilege of lust and luxury.

⋆ ⋆ ⋆ ⋆ ⋆ ⋆ ⋆ ⋆ ⋆ ⋆ ⋆ ⋆

from Chapter XVI

In the tenth year of the reign of Nero, the capital of the empire was afflicted by a fire which raged beyond the memory or example of former ages. The monuments of Grecian art and of Roman virtue, the trophies of the Punic and Gallic wars, the most holy temples, and the most splendid palaces, were involved in one common destruction. Of the fourteen regions or quarters into which Rome was divided, four only subsisted entire, three were levelled with the ground, and the remaining seven, which had experienced the fury of the flames, displayed a melancholy prospect of ruin and desolation. The vigilance of government appears not to have neglected any of the precautions which might alleviate the sense of so dreadful a calamity. The Imperial gardens were thrown open to the distressed multitude, temporary buildings were erected for their accommodation, and a plentiful supply of corn and provisions was distributed at a very moderate price. The most generous policy seemed to have dictated the edicts which regulated the disposition of the streets and the construction of private houses; and as it usually happens, in an age of prosperity, the conflagration of Rome, in the course of a few years, produced a new city, more regular and more beautiful than the former. But all the prudence and humanity affected by Nero on this occasion were insufficient to preserve him from the popular suspicion. Every crime might be imputed to the assassin of his wife and mother; nor could the prince, who prostituted his dignity and person on the theatre, be deemed incapable of the most extravagant folly. The voice of rumour accused the emperor as the incendiary of his own capital; and as the most incredible stories are the best adapted to the genius of an enraged people, it was gravely reported, and firmly believed, that Nero, enjoying the calamity which he had occasioned, amused himself with singing to his lyre the destruction of ancient Troy. To divert a suspicion, which the power of despotism was unable to suppress, the emperor resolved to substitute in his own place some fictitious criminals. 'With this view (continues Tacitus) he inflicted the most exquisite tortures on those men, who, under the vulgar appellation of Christians, were already branded with deserved infamy. They derived their name and origin from Christ, who in the reign of Tiberius had suffered death, by the sentence of the procurator Pontius Pilate. For a while, this dire superstition was checked; but it again burst forth; and not only spread itself over Judaea, the first seat of this mischievous sect, but was even introduced to Rome, the common asylum which receives and protects, whatever is impure, whatever is atrocious. The confessions of those who were seized, discovered a great multitude of their accomplices, and they were all convicted, not so much for the crime of setting fire to the city, as for their hatred of human kind. They died in torments, and their torments were embittered by insult and derision. Some were nailed on crosses; others sewn up in the skins of wild beasts, and exposed to the fury of dogs: others again, smeared over with combustible materials, were used as torches to illuminate the darkness of the night. The gardens of Nero were destined for the melancholy spectacle, which was accompanied with a horse race, and honoured with the presence of the emperor, who mingled with the populace in the dress and attitude of a charioteer. The guilt of the Christians deserved indeed the most exemplary punishment, but the public abhorrence was changed into commiseration, from the opinion that those unhappy wretches were sacrificed, not so much to the public welfare, as to the cruelty of a jealous tyrant.' Those who survey with a curious eye the revolutions of mankind, may observe, that the gardens and circus of Nero on the Vatican, which were polluted with the blood of the first Christians, have been rendered still more famous, by the triumph and by the abuse of the persecuted religion. On the same spot, a temple, which far surpasses the ancient glories of the Capitol, has been since erected by the Christian Pontiffs, who, deriving their claim of universal dominion from an humble fisherman of Galilee, have succeeded to the throne of the Caesars, given laws to the barbarian conquerors of Rome, and extended their spiritual jurisdiction from the coast of the Baltic to the shores of the Pacific Ocean.

## 3

## LINES WRITTEN DURING A PERIOD OF INSANITY

***William Cowper***

Hatred and vengeance, – my eternal portion
Scarce can endure delay of execution, –
Wait with impatient readiness to seize my
Soul in a moment.

Damn'd below Judas; more abhorr'd than he was,
Who for a few pence sold his holy Master!
Twice betray'd, Jesus me, the last delinquent,
Deems the profanest.

Man disavows, and Deity disowns me,
Hell might afford my miseries a shelter;
Therefore, Hell keeps her ever-hungry mouths all
Bolted against me.

Hard lot! encompassed with a thousand dangers;
Weary, faint, trembling with a thousand terrors,
I'm call'd, if vanquish'd! to receive a sentence
Worse than Abiram's.

Him the vindictive rod of angry Justice
Sent quick and howling to the centre headlong;
I, fed with judgment, in a fleshy tomb, am
Buried above ground.

## 4

## Extract from VATHEK

***William Beckford***

***translated by Samuel Henley***

Prayer at break of day was announced, when Carathis and Vathek ascended the steps which led to the summit of the tower, where they remained for some time though the weather was lowering and wet. This impending gloom corresponded with their malignant dispositions; but when the sun began to break through the clouds, they ordered a pavilion to be raised, as a screen against the intrusion of his beams. The Caliph, overcome with fatigue, sought refreshment from repose, at the same time hoping that significant dreams might attend on his slumbers; whilst the indefatigable Carathis, followed by a party of her mutes, descended to prepare whatever she judged proper for the oblation of the approaching night.

By secret stairs, contrived within the thickness of the wall, and known only to herself and her son, she first repaired to the mysterious recesses in which were deposited the mummies that had been wrested from the catacombs of the ancient Pharaohs. Of these she ordered several to be taken. From thence she resorted to a gallery where, under the guard of fifty female negroes, mute and blind of right eye, were preserved the oil of the most venomous serpents, rhinoceros' horns, and woods of a subtile and penetrating odour procured from the interior of the Indies, together with a thousand other horrible rarities. This collection had been formed for a purpose like the present, by Carathis herself, from a presentiment that she might one day enjoy some intercourse with the infernal powers, to whom she had ever been passionately attached, and to whose taste she was no stranger.

To familiarize herself the better with the horrors in view, the Princess remained in the company of her negresses, who squinted in the most amiable manner from the only eye they had, and leered, with exquisite delight, at the sculls and skeletons which Carathis had drawn forth from her cabinets: all of them making the most frightful contortions and uttering such shrill chatterings, that the Princess, stunned by them and suffocated by the potency of the exhalations, was forced to quit the gallery, after stripping it of a part of its abominable treasures.

Whilst she was thus occupied, the Caliph, who, instead of the visions he expected, had acquired in these unsubstantial regions a voracious appetite, was greatly provoked at the mutes. For having totally forgotten their deafness, he had impatiently asked them for food; and seeing them regardless of his demand, he began to cuff, pinch, and bite them, till Carathis arrived to terminate a scene so indecent, to the great content of these miserable creatures. 'Son! what means all this?' said she, panting for breath. 'I thought I heard as I came up the shrieks of a thousand bats, torn from their crannies in the recesses of a cavern; and it was the outcry only of these poor mutes, whom you were so unmercifully abusing. In truth, you but ill deserve the admirable provision I have brought you.' – 'Give it me instantly,' exclaimed the Caliph; 'I am perishing for hunger!' – 'As to that,' answered she, 'you must have an excellent stomach if it can digest what I have brought.' – 'Be quick,' replied the Caliph; – 'but, oh heavens! what horrors! what do you intend?' – 'Come, come,' returned Carathis, 'be not so squeamish; but help me to arrange every thing properly; and you shall see that what you reject with such symptoms of disgust will soon complete your felicity. Let us get ready the pile for the sacrifice of tonight; and think not of eating till that is performed: know you not, that all solemn rites ought to be preceded by a rigorous abstinence?'

The Caliph, not daring to object, abandoned himself to grief and the wind that ravaged his entrails, whilst his mother went forward with the requisite operations. Phials of serpents' oil, mummies, and bones, were soon set in order on the balustrade of the tower. The pile began to rise and in three hours was twenty cubits high. At length darkness approached, and

Carathis, having stripped herself to her inmost garment, clapped her hands in an impulse of ecstasy; the mutes followed her example; but Vathek, extenuated with hunger and impatience, was unable to support himself, and fell down in a swoon. The sparks had already kindled the dry wood; the venomous oil burst into a thousand blue flames; the mummies, dissolving, emitted a thick dun vapour; and the rhinoceros' horns, beginning to consume, all together diffused such a stench, that the Caliph, recovering, started from his trance, and gazed wildly on the scene in full blaze around him. The oil gushed forth in a plenitude of streams; and the negresses, who supplied it without intermission, united their cries to those of the Princess. At last the fire became so violent, and the flames reflected from the polished marble so dazzling, that the caliph, unable to withstand the heat and the blaze, effected his escape, and took shelter under the imperial standard.

In the mean time, the inhabitants of Samarah, scared at the light which shone over the city, arose in haste, ascended their roofs, beheld the tower on fire, and hurried, half naked, to the square. Their love for their sovereign immediately awoke; and, apprehending him in danger of perishing in his tower, their whole thoughts were occupied with the means of his safety. Morakanabad flew from his retirement, wiped away his tears, and cried out for water like the rest. Bababalouk, whose olfactory nerves were more familiarized to magical odours, readily conjecturing that Carathis was engaged in her favourite amusements, strenuously exhorted them not to be alarmed. Him, however, they treated as an old poltroon, and styled him a rascally traitor. The camels and dromedaries were advancing with water; but no one knew by which way to enter the tower. Whilst the populace was obstinate in forcing the doors, a violent north-east wind drove an immense volume of flame against them. At first they recoiled, but soon came back with redoubled zeal. At the same time, the stench of the horns and mummies increasing, most of the crowd fell backwards in a state of suffocation. Those that kept their feet mutually wondered at the cause of the smell, and admonished each other to retire. Morakanabad, more sick than the rest, remained in a piteous condition. Holding his nose with one hand, every one persisted in his efforts with the other to burst open the doors and obtain admission. A hundred and forty of the strongest and most resolute at length accomplished their purpose. Having gained the staircase, by their violent exertions, they attained a great height in a quarter of an hour.

Carathis, alarmed at the signs of her mutes, advanced to the staircase, went down a few steps, and heard several voices calling out from below, 'You shall in a moment have water!' Being rather alert, considering her age, she presently regained the top of the tower, and bade her son suspend the sacrifices for some minutes; adding, 'We shall soon be enabled to render it more grateful. Certain dolts of your subjects, imagining, no doubt, that we were on fire, have been rash enough to break through those doors which had hitherto remained inviolate, for the sake of bringing up water. They are very kind, you must allow, so soon to forget the wrongs you have done them; but that is of little moment. Let us offer them to the Giaour; let them come up; our mutes, who neither want strength nor experience, will soon dispatch them, exhausted as they are with fatigue.' – 'Be it so,' answered the Caliph, 'provided we finish, and I dine.' In fact, these good people, out of breath from ascending fifteen hundred stairs in such haste, and chagrined at having spilt by the way the water they had taken, were no sooner arrived at the top, than the blaze of the flames and the fumes of the mummies at once overpowered their senses. It was a pity! for they beheld not the agreeable smile with which the mutes and negresses adjusted the cord to their necks: these amiable personages rejoiced, however, no less at the scene. Never before had the ceremony of strangling been performed with so much facility. They all fell, without the least resistance of struggle: so that Vathek, in the space of a few moments, found himself surrounded by the dead bodies of the most faithful of his subjects; all of which were thrown on the top of the pile. Carathis, whose presence of mind never forsook her, perceiving that she had carcases sufficient to complete her oblation, commanded the chains to be stretched across the staircase, and the iron doors barricaded, that no more might come up.

No sooner were these orders obeyed, than the tower shook; the dead bodies vanished in the flames, which at once changed from a swarthy crimson to a bright rose colour; an ambient vapour emitted the most exquisite fragrance; the marble columns rang with harmonious sounds, and the liquefied horns diffused a delicious perfume. Carathis, in transports, anticipated the success of her enterprise; whilst her mutes and negresses, to whom these sweets had given the colic, retired grumbling to their cells.

Scarcely were they gone, when, instead of the pile, horns, mummies, and ashes, the Caliph both saw and felt, with a degree of pleasure which he could not express, a table covered with the most magnificent repast: flagons of wine and vases of exquisite sherbet reposing on snow. He availed himself, without scruple, of such an entertainment; and had already laid hands on a lamb stuffed with pistachios, whilst Carathis was privately drawing from a filigree urn a parchment that seemed to be endless, and which had escaped the notice of her son. Totally occupied in gratifying an importunate appetite, he left her to peruse it without interruption; which having finished, she said to him, in an authoritative tone, 'Put an end to your gluttony, and hear the splendid promises with which you are favoured!' She then read as follows: 'Vathek, my well-beloved, thou hast surpassed my hopes: my nostrils have been regaled by the savour of thy mummies, thy horns, and, still more, by the lives devoted on the pile. At the full of the moon, cause the bands of thy musicians, and thy tymbals, to be heard; depart from thy palace, surrounded by all the pageants of majesty – thy most faithful slaves, thy best beloved wives, thy most magnificent litters, thy richest loaden camels – and set forward on thy way to Ishtakar. There I await thy coming: that is the region of wonders: there shalt thou receive the diadem of Gian Ben Gian, the talismans of Soliman, and the treasures of the pre-Adamite sultans: there shalt thou be solaced with all kinds of delight. – But beware how thou enterest any dwelling on thy route; or thou shalt feel the effects of my anger.'

The Caliph, notwithstanding his habitual luxury, had never before dined with so much satisfaction. He gave full scope to the joy of these golden tidings; and betook himself to drinking anew. Carathis, whose antipathy to wine was by no means insuperable, failed not to pledge him at every bumper he ironically quaffed to the health of Mahomet. This infernal liquor completed their impious temerity, and prompted them to utter a profusion of blasphemies. They gave a loose to their wit, at the expense of the ass of Balaam, the dog of the seven sleepers, and the other animals admitted into the Paradise of Mahomet. In this sprightly humour, they descended the fifteen hundred stairs, diverting themselves as they went, at the anxious faces they saw on the square, through the barbicans and loopholes of the tower; and at length arrived at the royal apartments, by the subterranean passage. Bababalouk was parading to and fro, and issuing his mandates with great pomp to the eunuchs, who were snuffing the lights and painting the eyes of the Circassians. No sooner did he catch sight of the Caliph and his mother, than he exclaimed, 'Hah! you have then, I perceive, escaped from the flames; I was not, however, altogether out of doubt.' – 'Of what moment is it to us what you thought or think?' cried Carathis: 'go, speed; tell Morakanabad that we immediately want him; and take care not to stop by the way to make your insipid reflections.'

Morakanabad delayed not to obey the summons, and was received by Vathek and his mother with great solemnity. They told him, with an air of composure and commiseration, that the fire at the top of the tower was extinguished; but that it had cost the lives of the brave people who sought to assist them.

'Still more misfortunes!' cried Morakanabad, with a sigh. 'Ah, commander of the faithful, our holy Prophet is certainly irritated against us! it behoves you to appease him.' 'We will appease him hereafter,' replied the Caliph, with a smile that augured nothing good. 'You will have leisure sufficient for your supplications during my absence, for this country is the bane of my health. I am disgusted with the mountain of the four fountains, and am resolved to go and drink of the stream of Rocnabad. I long to refresh myself in the delightful valleys which it waters. Do you, with the advice of my mother, govern my dominions, and take care to supply whatever her experiments may demand; for you well know that our tower abounds in materials for the advancement of science.'

The tower but ill suited Morakanabad's taste. Immense treasures had been lavished upon it; and nothing had he ever seen carried thither but female negroes, mutes, and abominable drugs. Nor did he know well what to think of Carathis, who, like a cameleon, could assume all possible colours. Her cursed eloquence had often driven the poor Mussulman to his last shifts. He considered, however, that if she possessed but few good qualities, her son had still fewer; and that the alternative, on the whole, would be in her favour. Consoled, therefore, with this reflection, he went, in good spirits, to soothe the populace, and make the proper arrangements for his master's journey.

Vathek, to conciliate the spirits of the subterranean palace, resolved that his expedition should be uncommonly splendid. With this view he confiscated, on all sides, the property of his subjects; whilst his worthy mother stripped the seraglios she visited of the gems they contained. She collected all the sempstresses and embroiderers of Samarah and other cities, to the distance of sixty leagues, to prepare pavilions, palanquins, sofas, canopies, and litters for the train of the monarch. There was not left, in Masulipatan, a single piece of chintz; and so much muslin had been brought up to dress out Bababalouk and the other black eunuchs, that there remained not an ell of it in the whole Irak of Babylon.

During these preparations, Carathis, who never lost sight of her great object, which was to obtain favour with the powers of darkness, made select parties of the fairest and most delicate ladies of the city; but in the midst of their gaiety, she contrived to introduce vipers amongst them, and to break pots of scorpions under the table. They all bit to a wonder, and Carathis would have left her friends to die, were it not that, to fill up the time, she now and then amused herself in curing their wounds, with an excellent anodyne of her own invention: for this good Princess abhorred being indolent.

Vathek, who was not altogether so active as his mother, devoted his time to the sole gratification of his senses, in the palaces which were severally dedicated to them. He disgusted himself no more with the divan, or the mosque. One half of Samarah followed his example, whilst the other lamented the progress of corruption.

## 5

## DARKNESS

### *Lord Byron*

I had a dream, which was not all a dream.
The bright sun was extinguish'd, and the stars
Did wander darkling in the eternal space,
Rayless, and pathless, and the icy earth
Swung blind and blackening in the moonless air;
Morn came and went – and came, and brought no day,
And men forgot their passions in the dread
Of this their desolation; and all hearts
Were chill'd into a selfish prayer for light:
And they did live by watchfires – and the thrones,
The palaces of crowned kings – the huts,
The habitations of all things which dwell,
Were burnt for beacons; cities were consumed,
And men were gathered round their blazing homes
To look once more into each other's face;
Happy were those who dwelt within the eye
Of the volcanos, and their mountain-torch:
A fearful hope was all the world contain'd;
Forests were set on fire – but hour by hour
They fell and faded – and the crackling trunks
Extinguish'd with a crash – and all was black.
The brows of men by the despairing light
Wore an unearthly aspect, as by fits
The flashes fell upon them; some lay down
And hid their eyes and wept; and some did rest
Their chins upon their clenched hands, and smiled;
And others hurried to and fro, and fed
Their funeral piles with fuel, and look'd up
With mad disquietude on the dull sky,
The pall of a past world; and then again
With curses cast them down upon the dust,

And gnash'd their teeth and howl'd: the wild birds
shriek'd
And, terrified, did flutter on the ground,
And flap their useless wings; the wildest brutes
Came tame and tremulous; and vipers crawl'd
And twined themselves among the multitude,
Hissing, but stingless – they were slain for food.
And War, which for a moment was no more,
Did glut himself again: – a meal was bought
With blood, and each sate sullenly apart
Gorging himself in gloom: no love was left;
All earth was but one thought – and that was death
Immediate and inglorious; and the pang
Of famine fed upon all entrails – men
Died, and their bones were tombless as their flesh;
The meagre by the meagre were devour'd,
Even dogs assail'd their masters, all save one,
And he was faithful to a corse, and kept
The birds and beasts and famish'd men at bay,
Till hunger clung them, or the dropping dead
Lured their lank jaws; himself sought out no food,
But with a piteous and perpetual moan,
And a quick desolate cry, licking the hand
Which answer'd not with a caress – he died.
The crowd was famish'd by degrees; but two
Of an enormous city did survive,
And they were enemies: they met beside
The dying embers of an altar-place
Where had been heap'd a mass of holy things
For an unholy usage; they raked up,
And shivering scraped with their cold skeleton hands
The feeble ashes, and their feeble breath
Blew for a little life, and made a flame
Which was a mockery; then they lifted up
Their eyes as it grew lighter, and beheld
Each other's aspects – saw, and shriek'd and died –
Even of their mutual hideousness they died,
Unknowing who he was upon whose brow

Famine had written Fiend. The world was void,
The populous and the powerful was a lump,
Seasonless, herbless, treeless, manless, lifeless,
A lump of death – a chaos of hard clay.
The rivers, lakes and ocean all stood still,
And nothing stirr'd within their silent depths;
Ships sailorless lay rotting on the sea,
And their masts fell down piecemeal: as they dropp'd
They slept on the abyss without a surge –
The waves were dead; the tides were in their grave,
The moon, their mistress, had expired before;
The winds were wither'd in the stagnant air,
And the clouds perish'd: Darkness had no need
Of aid from them – She was the Universe.

## 6

## A DREAM

***Bryan Waller Procter ('Barry Cornwall')***

The night was gloomy. Through the skies of June
Rolled the eternal moon.
Midst dark and heavy clouds that bore
A shadowy likeness to those fabled things
That sprung of old from man's imaginings.
Each seemed a fierce reality; some wore
The forms of sphinx and hippogriff, or seemed
Nourished among the wonders of the deep,
And wilder than the poet ever dreamed;
And there were cars – steeds with their proud necks
    bent;
Tower, and temple, and broken continent;
And all, as upon a sea,
In the blue ether floated silently.
I lay upon my bed and sank to sleep;
And then I fancied that I rode upon
The waters, and had power to call
Up people who had lived in ages gone,
And scenes and stories half-forgot – and all
That on my young imagination
Had come like fairy visions, and departed.
And ever by me a broad current passed
Slowly, from which at times up started
Dim scenes and ill-defined shapes. At last
I bade the billows render up their dead,
And all their wild inhabitants; and I
Summoned the spirits who perished,
Or took their stations in the starry sky,
When Jove himself bowed his Saturnian head
Before the One Divinity.

First I saw a landscape fair
Towering in the clear blue air,
Like Ida's woody summits, and sweet fields,
Where all that nature yields
Flourishes. Three proud shapes were seen,
Standing upon the green
Like Olympian queens descended.
One was unadorned, and one
Wore her golden tresses bound
With simple flowers; the third was crowned,
And from amidst her raven hair,
Like stars, imperial jewels shone.
Not one of those figures divine
But might have sat in Juno's chair,
And smiled in great equality
On Jove, though the blue skies were shaken;
Or, with superior aspect, taken
From Hebe's hand nectarean wine.
And that Dardanian boy was there
Whom pale Oenone loved; his hair
Was black, and curled his temples round;
His limbs were free and his forehead fair,
And, as he stood on a rising ground,
And back his dark locks proudly tossed,
A shepherd youth he looked, but trod
On the green sward like a god –
Most like Apollo when he played,
'Fore Midas, in the Phrygian shade,
With Pan, and to the Sylvan lost.

And now from out the watery floor
A city rose (and well she wore
Her beauty), and stupendous walls,
And towers that touched the stars, and halls
Pillared with whitest marble, whence
Palace on lofty palace sprung;
And over all rich gardens hung,
Where, amongst silver waterfalls,

Cedars and spice-trees and green bowers,
And sweet winds playing with all the flowers
Of Persia and of Araby,
Walked princely shapes; some with an air
Like warriors, some like ladies fair
Listening, and, amidst all, the king
Nebuchadnezzar rioting
In supreme magnificence.
This was famous Babylon.

That glorious vision passed on.
And then I heard the laurel-branches sigh
That still grow where the bright-eyed muses walked;
And Pelion shook his piny locks, and talked
Mournfully to the fields of Thessaly.
And there I saw, piercing the deep blue sky,
And radiant with his diadem of snow,
Crowned Olympus; and the hills below
Looked like inferior spirits tending round
His pure supremacy; and a sound
Went rolling onwards through the sunny calm,
As if immortal voices then had spoken,
And, with rich noises, broken
The silence which that holy place had bred.
I knelt – and as I knelt, haply in token
Of thanks, there fell a honeyed shower of balm,
And then came one who on the Nubian sands
Perished for love; and with him the wanton queen
Egyptian in her state was seen;
And how she smiled, and kissed his willing hands,
And said she would not love, and swore to die,
And laughed upon the Roman Antony.
Oh matchless Cleopatra! never since
Has one, and never more
Shall one like thee tread on the Egyptian shore,
Or lavish such royal magnificence;
Never shall one laugh, love or die like thee,
Or own so sweet a witchery;

And, brave Mark Antony, that thou could'st give
Half the wide world to live
With that enchantress, did become thee well;
For love is wiser than ambition:
Queen and thou, lofty triumvir, fare ye well.

And then I heard the sullen waters roar,
And saw them cast their surf upon the strand,
And then, rebounding toward some far-seen land,
They washed and washed its melancholy shore,
And the terrific spirits, bred
In the sea-caverns, moved by those fierce jars,
Rose up like giants from their watery bed,
And shook their silver hair against the stars.
Then bursts like thunder, joyous outcries wild
Sounds as from trumpets, and from drums,
And music, like the lulling noise that comes
From nurses when they hush their charge to sleep,
Came in confusion from the deep.
Methought one told me that a child
Was that night unto the great Neptune born;
And then old Triton blew his curled horn,
And the Leviathan lashed the foaming seas,
And the wanton nereides
Came up like phantoms from their coral halls,
And laughed and sung like tipsy Bacchanals,
Till all the fury of the ocean broke
Upon my ear. I trembled and awoke.

# 7

## Passages from THE STORY OF PRINCE ALASI AND THE PRINCESS FIROUZKAH

***William Beckford***
***translated by Sir Frank Marzials***

. . . I looked round on every side, and it seemed to me I was in a vast plain, and that round it were transparent clouds, which held enfolded, not only ourselves, but all the most beautiful and delicious products of the earth. 'Ah!' cried I, after a moment of surprise, and embracing Firouzkah, 'what is it to us if we have been carried into Cheristan itself! The true realms of bliss are in thine arms!'

'This is not Cheristan,' replied the daughter of Filanshaw. 'It is only the Mage's cave, which an infinite number of Beings, superior to our race, take pleasure in decorating with a varied beauty. But such as it is, and whatever may be its inhabitants, everything will be done here to anticipate your wishes. Is it not so, my Father?' continued she, raising her voice.

'Undoubtedly,' replied the Mage, appearing suddenly before our eyes, and advancing towards me with a smile. 'Prince Alasi will be treated here as he has treated my dear Firouzkah; and, moreover, the priceless jewel I confided to his care – Firouzkah herself – shall be his to possess for ever, if such be his desire. Come, let the marriage feast be at once prepared, and all things made ready for so great an event!'

He had no sooner spoken these words, than the cavern again changed its aspect. It assumed an oval shape, and diminished proportions, and appeared all encrusted with pale sapphires. Round us, on divans, were ranged boy and girl musicians, who charmed our ears with melodious strains, while from their heads, light-encircled, shone rays more pure and soft than would be shed by a thousand tapers.

We were placed at a table covered with excellent dainties

and the most exquisite wines, and were served delightfully by Persian boys and by Georgian girls – all as white and graceful as the jasmine sprays engarlanding their fair heads. With their every motion the gauze robes, that half clothed half revealed them, exhaled the sweetest perfumes of Araby the Blest. Firouzkah, who could not at once forget her part as Firouz, sported with these children as they filled our cups, and indulged in a thousand pranks.

★ ★ ★ ★ ★ ★ ★ ★ ★ ★ ★ ★

Firouzkah had no desire for sleep, and related to me how, in a moment, the Mage had healed her wound. She vaunted his power, and advised that I should ask him to show me his Hall of Fire, confessing that she herself had been brought up in the religion of Zoroaster, and considered it the most natural and rational of all religions. 'Think, then,' she added, 'if I could ever have taken delight in the absurdities of the Koran. Would that all your Mussulman doctors had shared the fate of the Mullah whose discourses wearied me to death! That moment was indeed delicious when I induced him to put on the outward seeming of an ass. I should have taken a like pleasure in plucking out all the feathers from the wings of the Angel Gabriel, and thus punishing him for having furnished a pen to the man who wrote therewith so much nonsense, – if indeed I had been simpleton enough to believe that absurd story.'

There was a time when such words would have seemed to me unspeakable for their very wickedness; and in good sooth I did not like them much then. But any remaining scruples formed but a weak defence against the alluring caresses with which Firouzkah accompanied her every word.

A voluptuous sleep enveloped us at last; and we did not wake till the lively song of birds proclaimed broad day.

Surprised by sounds which I had no reason to expect in such a place, I ran to the grotto's entrance, and found it led to a garden containing all that is most delightful in nature, while the encircling sea enhanced the beauties which the earth exhibited to our gaze.

'Is this another illusion?' I asked, 'for this, at least, cannot be part of the Mage's cavern?'

'It is one of its issues,' replied Firouzkah; 'but it would take you more than one day to explore all the beauties of the place. The Mage says that everything has been made for man's use, and that man must possess himself of everything he wants when ever the opportunity offers. He has spent part of his life in acquiring his power, and is spending the remainder in enjoying its fruits.'

I did not fail to express to the Mage a very strong desire to see his Hall of Fire. 'It will please you,' said he, with a satisfied air; 'but I cannot conduct you thither until you have visited my baths, and been invested with robes suitable to the majesty of the place.'

To please Firouzkah I consented to everything that was demanded of me; and, for fear of offending her, I even refrained from laughter at the grotesque robes in which we were both ridiculously accoutred. But what were my feelings, on entering the Hall of Fire? Never has a spectacle so filled me with surprise and terror – never, until overwhelmed by the sight that met my eyes on entering the fatal place in which we now are!

The fire that the Mage worshipped seemed to issue from the bowels of the earth and to soar above the clouds. The flames sometimes shone with an unendurable brightness; sometimes they shed a blue and lurid light, making all surrounding objects appear even more hideous than they actually were. The rails of glowing brass that separated us from this dread deity did no more than partially reassure me. From time to time we were enveloped in a whirlwind of sparks, which the Mage regarded as graciously emitted in our honour – an honour with which I would very gladly have dispensed. In the portion of the temple where we stood, the walls were hung with human hair of every colour; and, from space to space, human hair hung also in festoons from pyramids of skulls chased in gold and ebony. Besides all this, the place was filled with the fumes of sulphur and bitumen, oppressing the brain and taking away the breath. I trembled; my legs seemed to give way; Firouzkah supported me. 'Take me hence,' I whispered; 'take me from the sight of thy god. Nothing save thine own presence has enabled me to endure *his* presence for a moment!'

It was some time before I fully recovered. In order to effect my restoration, the Dives introduced a fresher air through orifices in the vault of the cavern where we had supped the night before. They also redecorated the cavern itself in a novel manner, and prepared for us an exquisite repast. I was thus enabled to listen to the Mage with renewed patience. What my terrible host told me about his religion did not indeed possess the charms of novelty: I knew most of it before, and I paid small heed to this part of his discourse. But his moral teachings pleased me hugely, since they flattered passion and abolished remorse. He greatly vaunted his Hall of Fire – told us that the Dives had built it, but that he himself had supplied the decorations at the risk of his life. I asked him for no explanation on this point; I was even afraid lest he should give them unasked. I could not think of those skulls, of that human hair, of what he called 'decorations' without trembling. I should have feared the worst in that dreadful place if I had not been so sure of the heart of Firouzkah.

Fortunately I was not called upon to listen to the Mage's discourses more than once a day. The rest of our time was spent in amusements and pleasures of every kind. These the Dives never failed to supply; and Firouzkah caused them to gratify my every taste by an infinite variety. Her assiduous care, her ingenuity of tenderness, made my every moment hurry by in such voluptuous enjoyment that I was never to measure the flight of time; and the present had so far obliterated the past that I never once thought of my kingdom. But the Mage put an end, all too soon, alas! to this period of delirium and enchantment. One day, one fatal day, he said to us: 'We are about to separate, my dear children; the hour of bliss, for which I have sighed for such long years, is approaching; I am expected in the Palace of Subterranean Fire, where I shall bathe in joys untold, and possess treasures surpassing man's imagination. Ah! why has this moment of supreme felicity been so long delayed? The inexorable hand of death would not then have torn from my side my dear Soudabe, whose charms had never suffered from the ravages of Time! We should then have partaken together of that perfect happiness which neither accident, nor the vicissitudes of life, can ever mar in the place to which I am bound.'

'Ah!' I cried, 'where is that divine sojourn in which a happy eternity of mutual love and tenderness may be enjoyed? Let us follow you thither.'

'You may do so, if you worship my god,' replied the Mage; 'if you will do homage to the powers that serve him, if you will win his favour by such sacrifices as he ordains.'

'I will worship any god you like,' said I, 'if he will suffer me to live forever with Firouzkah, and free from the horrible fear of seeing pale disease or bloody steel threaten her beauteous life. What must I do besides?'

'You must,' replied the Mage, 'cause the religion of Zoroaster to be received in your dominions, raze the mosques to the ground, erect Halls of Fire in their stead, and, finally, sacrifice without pity all whom you cannot convert to the true faith. This is what I have myself done, though not so openly as you can do it; and, as a sign of what I have been able to accomplish, see all these locks of hair that ornament my Hall of Fire – dear evidences that I am about to enter the gates of the only place where lasting joys are to be found.'

'Quick, quick! let us go and cause heads to be cut off,' said Firouzkah, 'and so amass a treasure of human hair! You will agree, my dear Alasi, that the sacrifice of a whole tribe of crazy wretches who will not accept our belief, is as nothing if we can obtain thereby the supreme felicity of loving each other for all time!'

By these flattering words Firouzkah obtained my complete assent, and the Mage, having reached the height of his wishes, resumed: 'I esteem myself happy, King of Kharezme, in seeing you, at last, convinced of the truth of my faith. Several times have I despaired, and I should certainly not have taken so much trouble about you if you had not been the husband of the daughter of Filanshaw – my friend and disciple. Ah! what honour will be mine when your conversion is known in the Palace of Subterranean Fire! Hence, therefore! Depart at once. A ship, ready equipped, awaits you upon the shore. Your subjects will receive you with acclamation. Do all the good you can. Remember that to destroy those who are obstinate in error is accounted a great merit by the stern god you have promised to serve. When you deem that your reward is fully earned, go to Istakhar, and there, on the Terrace of the Beacon Lights, make a holocaust of the hair of those whom you have immolated in so good a cause. The nostrils of the Dives will be gratified by that sweet-smelling sacrifice. They will discover to you the steep and secret stairway, and open the ebony portals: I shall receive you in my arms, and see that you are received with fitting honours.'

Thus did I yield to the last seductions of the Mage.

# 8

## Verses from
## CHILDE HAROLD'S PILGRIMAGE: A ROMAUNT
***Lord Byron***

from Canto I.

II

Whilome in Albion's isle there dwelt a youth,
Who ne in virtue's ways did take delight;
But spent his days in riot most uncouth,
And vexed with mirth the drowsy ear of night.
Ah, me! in sooth he was a shameless wight,
Sore given to revel and ungodly glee;
Few earthly things found favour in his sight
Save concubines and carnal companie,
And flaunting wassailers of high and low degree.

III

Childe Harold was he hight: – but whence his name
And lineage long, it suits me not to say;
Suffice it, that perchance they were of fame,
And had been glorious in another day:
But one sad losel soils a name for aye,
However mighty in the olden time;
Nor all that heralds rake from coffined clay,
Nor florid prose, nor honied lines of rhyme,
Can blazon evil deeds, or consecrate a crime.

IV

Childe Harold basked him in the noontide sun,
Disporting there like any other fly;
Nor deemed before his little day was done

One blast might chill him into misery.
But long ere scarce a third of his passed by
Worse than adversity the Childe befell;
He felt the fulness of satiety:
Then loathed he in his native land to dwell,
Which seemed to him more lone than Eremite's sad
cell.

V

For he through Sin's long labyrinth had run,
Nor made atonement when he did amiss,
Had sighed to many though he loved but one,
And that loved one, alas! could ne'er be his.
Ah, happy she! to 'scape from him whose kiss
Had been pollution unto aught so chaste;
Who soon had left her charms for vulgar bliss,
And spoiled her goodly lands to gild his waste,
Nor calm domestic peace had ever deigned to taste.

VI

And now Childe Harold was sore sick at heart,
And from his fellow bacchanals would flee;
'Tis said, at times the sullen tear would start,
But pride congealed the drop within his ee:
Apart he stalked in joyless reverie,
And from his native land resolved to go,
And visit scorching climes beyond the sea;
With pleasure drugged, he almost longed for woe,
And e'en for change of scene would seek the shades
below.

VII

The Childe departed from his father's hall:
It was a vast and venerable pile;
So old, it seemèd only not to fall,

Yet strength was pillared in each massy aisle.
Monastic dome! condemned to uses vile!
Where superstition once had made her den
Now Paphian girls were known to sing and smile;
And monks might deem their time was come agen,
If ancient tales say true, nor wrong these holy men.

VIII

Yet oft-times in his maddest mirthful mood
Strange pangs would flash along Childe Harold's brow,
As if the memory of some deadly feud
Or disappointed passion lurked below:
But this none knew, nor haply cared to know;
For his was not that open, artless soul
That feels relief by bidding sorrow flow,
Nor sought he friend to counsel or condole
Whate'er this grief mote be, which he could not control.

IX

And none did love him! – though to hall and bower
He gathered revellers from far and near,
He knew them flatterers of the festal hour;
The heartless parasites of present cheer.
Yea! none did love him – not his lemans dear –
But pomp and power alone are woman's care,
And where these are light Eros finds a feere;
Maidens, like moths, are ever caught by glare,
And Mammon wins his way where Seraphs might despair.

X

Childe Harold had a mother – not forgot,
Though parting from that mother he did shun;

A sister whom he loved, but saw her not
Before his weary pilgrimage begun:
If friends he had, he bade adieu to none.
Yet deem not thence his breast a breast of steel:
Ye, who have known what 'tis to dote upon
A few dear objects, will in sadness feel
Such partings break the heart they fondly hope to heal.

XI

His house, his home, his heritage, his lands,
The laughing dames in whom he did delight,
Whose large blue eyes, fair locks and snowy hands,
Might shake the saintship of an anchorite,
And long had fed his youthful appetite;
His goblets brimmed with every costly wine,
And all that mote to luxury invite,
Without a sigh, he left to cross the brine,
And traverse Paynim shores, and pass Earth's central line.

* * * * * * * * * * * *

from Canto IV.

CVIII

There is the moral of all human tales;
'Tis but the same rehearsal of the past,
First Freedom, and then Glory – when that fails,
Wealth, vice, corruption, – barbarism at last.
And History, with all her volumes vast,
Hath but *one* page, – 'tis better written here,
Where gorgeous Tyranny hath thus amassed
All treasures, all delights, that eye or ear,
Heart, soul could seek, tongue ask – away with words!
draw near,

## CIX

Admire, exult – despise – laugh, weep, – for here
There is such matter for all feeling: – Man!
Thou pendulum betwixt a smile and tear,
Ages and realms are crowded in this span,
This mountain, whose obliterated plan
The pyramid of empires pinnacled,
Of Glory's gewgaws shining in the van
Till the sun's rays with added flame were filled!
Where are its golden roofs? Where those who dared to
build?

## 9

## ON THE MEDUSA OF LEONARDO DA VINCI IN THE FLORENTINE GALLERY

***Percy Bysshe Shelley***

It lieth, gazing on the midnight sky,
   Upon the cloudy mountain peak supine;
Below, far lands are seen tremblingly;
   Its horror and its beauty are divine.
Upon its lips and eyelids seem to lie
   Loveliness like a shadow, from which shrine,
Fiery and lurid, struggling underneath,
The agonies of anguish and of death.

Yet it is less the horror than the grace
   Which turns the gazer's spirit into stone
Whereon the lineaments of that dead face
   Are graven, till the characters be grown
Into itself, and thought no more can trace;
   'Tis the melodious hues of beauty thrown
Athwart the darkness and the glare of pain,
Which humanised and harmonize the strain.

And from its head as from one body grow,
   As [ ] grass out of a watery rock,
Hairs which are vipers, and they curl and flow,
   And their long tangles in each other lock,
And with unending involutions show
   Their mailed radiance, as it were to mock
The torture and the death within, and saw
The solid air with many a ragged jaw.

And from a stone beside, a poisonous eft
   Peeps idly into these Gorgonian eyes;
Whilst in the air a ghastly bat, bereft
   Of sense, has flitted with a mad surprise

Out of the cave this hideous light hath cleft,
   And he comes hastening like a moth that hies
After a taper; and the midnight sky
Flares, a light more dread than obscurity.

'Tis the tempestuous loveliness of terror;
   For from the serpents gleams a brazen glare
Kindled by that inextricable error,
   Which makes a thrilling vapour of the air
Become a [ ] and ever-shifting mirror
   Of all the beauty and the terror there –
A woman's countenance, with serpent locks,
Gazing in death on heaven from those wet rocks.

## 10

## Verses from ENDYMION: A POETIC ROMANCE

*John Keats*

Bk. III, ll.477–554

'One morn she left me sleeping: half awake
I sought for her smooth arms and lips, to slake
My greedy thirst with nectarous camel-draughts;
But she was gone. Whereat the barbed shafts
Of disappointment stuck in me so sore,
That out I ran and search'd the forest o'er.
Wandering about in pine and cedar gloom
Damp awe assail'd me; for there 'gan to boom
A sound of moan, an agony of sound,
Sepulchral from the distance all around.
Then came a conquering earth-thunder, and rumbled
That fierce complain to silence: while I stumbled
Down a precipitous path, as if impell'd.
I came to a dark valley. – Groanings swell'd
Poisonous about my ears, and louder grew,
The nearer I approach'd a flame's gaunt blue,
That glar'd before me through a thorny brake
This fire, like the eye of a gordian snake,
Bewitch'd me towards; and I soon was near
A sight too fearful for the feel of fear.
In thicket hid I curs'd the haggard scene –
The banquet of my arms, my arbour queen,
Seated upon an uptorn forest root;
And all around her shapes, wizard and brute,
Laughing, and wailing, groveling, serpenting,
Showing tooth, tusk, and venom-bag, and sting!
O such deformities! Old Charon's self,
Should he give up awhile his penny pelf,

And take a dream 'mongst rushes Stygian,
It could not be so phantasied. Fierce, wan,
And tyrannizing was the lady's look,
As over them a gnarled staff she shook.
Oft-times upon the sudden she laugh'd out,
And from a basket emptied to the rout
Clusters of grapes, the which they raven'd quick
And roar'd for more; with many a hungry lick
About their shaggy jaws. Avenging, slow,
Anon she took a branch of mistletoe,
And emptied on't a black dull-gurgling phial:
Groan'd one and all, as if some piercing trial
Was sharpening for their pitiable bones.
She lifted up the charm: appealing groans
From their poor breasts went sueing to her ear
In vain; remorseless as an infant's bier
She whisk'd against their eyes the sooty oil.
Whereat was heard a noise of painful toil,
Increasing gradual to a tempest rage,
Shrieks, yells, and groans of torture-pilgrimage;
Until their grieved bodies 'gan to bloat
And puff from the tail's end to stifled throat:
Then was appalling silence: then a sight
More wildering than all that hoarse affright;
For the whole herd, as by a whirlwind writhen,
Went through the dismal air like one huge Python
Antagonizing Boreas, – and so vanish'd.
Yet there was not a breath of wind: she banish'd
These phantoms with a nod. Lo! from the dark
Came waggish fauns, and nymphs, and satyrs stark,
With dancing and loud revelry, – and went
Swifter than centaurs after rapine bent. –
Sighing an elephant appear'd and bow'd
Before the fierce witch, speaking thus aloud
In human accent: 'Potent goddess! chief
Of pains resistless! make my being brief,
Or let me from this heavy prison fly:
Or give me to the air, or let me die!

I sue not for my happy crown again;
I sue not for my phalanx on the plain;
I sue not for my lone, my widow'd wife;
I sue not for my ruddy drops of life,
My children fair, my lovely girls and boys!
I will forget them; I will pass these joys;
Ask nought so heavenward, so too – too high:
Only I pray, as fairest boon, to die,
Or be deliver'd from this cumbrous flesh,
From this gross, detestable, filthy mesh,
And merely given to the cold bleak air.
Have mercy, Goddess! Circe, feel my prayer!'

★ ★ ★ ★ ★ ★ ★ ★ ★ ★ ★ ★

Bk. IV, ll. 513–542

There lies a den,
Beyond the seeming confines of the space
Made for the soul to wander in and trace
Its own existence, of remotest glooms.
Dark regions are around it, where the tombs
Of buried griefs the spirit sees, but scarce
One hour doth linger weeping, for the pierce
Of new-born woe it feels more inly smart:
And in these regions many a venom'd dart
At random flies; they are the proper home
Of every ill: the man is yet to come
Who hath not journeyed in this native hell.
But few have ever felt how calm and well
Sleep may be had in that deep den of all.
There anguish does not sting; nor pleasure pall:
Woe-hurricanes beat ever at the gate,
Yet all is still within and desolate.
Beset with plainful gusts, within ye hear
No sound so loud as when on curtain'd bier
The death-watch tick is stifled. Enter none
Who strive therefore: on the sudden it is won.
Just when the sufferer begins to burn,

Then it is free to him; and from an urn,
Still fed by melting ice, he takes a draught –
Young Semele such richness never quaft
In her maternal longing! Happy gloom!
Dark Paradise! where pale becomes the bloom
Of health by due; where silence dreariest
Is most articulate; where hopes infest;
Where those eyes are the brightest far that keep
Their lids shut longest in a dreamless sleep.

## 11

## Verses from THE GIAOUR

***Lord Byron***

ll. 747–786

But thou, false Infidel! shalt writhe
Beneath avenging Monkir's scythe;
And from its torment 'scape alone
To wander round lost Eblis' throne;
And fire unquench'd, unquenchable,
Around, within thy heart shall dwell;
Nor ear can hear nor tongue can tell
The tortures of that inward hell!
But first, on earth as Vampire sent,
Thy corse shall from its tomb be rent:
Then ghastly haunt thy native place,
And suck the blood of all thy race;
There from thy daughter, sister, wife,
At midnight drain the stream of life;
Yet loathe the banquet which perforce
Must feed thy living livid corse;
Thy victims ere they yet expire
Shall know the demon for their sire,
As cursing thee, thou cursing them,
Thy flowers are wither'd on the stem.
But one that for thy crime must fall,
The youngest, most beloved of all,
Shall bless thee with a *father's* name –
That word shall wrap thy heart in flame!
Yet must thou end thy task, and mark
Her cheek's last tinge, her eye's last spark,
And the last glassy glance must view
Which freezes o'er its lifeless blue;
Then with unhallow'd hand shalt tear

The tresses of her yellow hair,
Of which in life a lock when shorn,
Affection's fondest pledge was worn,
But now is borne away by thee,
Memorial of thine agony!
Wet with thine own best blood shall drip
Thy gnashing tooth and haggard lip;
Then stalking to thy sullen grave,
Go – and with Gouls and Afrits rave;
Till these in horror shrink away
From spectre more accursed than they!

★ ★ ★ ★ ★ ★ ★ ★ ★ ★ ★ ★

ll. 937–970

If solitude succeed to grief,
Release from pain is slight relief;
The vacant bosom's wilderness
Might thank the pang that made it less.
We loathe what none are left to share:
Even bliss – 'twere woe alone to bear;
The heart once thus left desolate
Must fly at last for ease – to hate.
It is as if the dead could feel
The icy worm around them steal,
And shudder, as the reptiles creep
To revel o'er their rotting sleep,
Without the power to scare away
The cold consumers of their clay!
It is as if the desert bird,
  Whose beak unlocks her bosom's stream
  To still her famish'd nestlings' scream,
Nor mourns a life to them transferr'd,
Should rend her rash devoted breast,
And find them flown her empty nest.
The keenest pangs the wretched find
  Are rapture to the dreary void,
The leafless desert of the mind,

The waste of feelings unemploy'd.
Who would be doom'd to gaze upon
A sky without a cloud or sun?
Less hideous far the tempest's roar
Than ne'er to brave the billows more –
Thrown, when the war of winds is o'er,
A lonely wreck on fortune's shore,
'Mid sullen calm, and silent bay,
Unseen to drop by dull decay; –
Better to sink beneath the shock
Than moulder piecemeal on the rock!

# 12

## Extract from
## CONFESSIONS OF AN ENGLISH OPIUM-EATER
### *Thomas De Quincey*

. . . All this, and much more than I can say, or have time to say, the reader must enter into before he can comprehend the unimaginable horror which these dreams of oriental imagery, and mythological tortures, impressed upon me. Under the connecting feeling of tropical heat and vertical sunlights, I brought together all creatures, birds, beasts, reptiles, all trees and plants, usages and appearances, that are found in all tropical regions, and assembled them together in China or Indostan. From kindred feelings, I soon brought Egypt and all her gods under the same law. I was stared at, hooted at, grinned at, chattered at, by monkeys, by paroquets, by cockatoos. I ran into pagodas: and was fixed, for centuries, at the summit, or in secret rooms; I was the idol; I was the priest; I was worshipped; I was sacrificed. I fled from the wrath of Brama through all the forests of Asia: Vishnu hated me: Seeva laid wait for me. I came suddenly upon Isis and Osiris: I had done a deed, they said, which the ibis and the crocodile trembled at. I was buried, for a thousand years, in stone coffins, with mummies and sphynxes, in narrow chambers at the heart of eternal pyramids. I was kissed, with cancerous kisses, by crocodiles; and laid, confounded with all unutterable slimy things, amongst reeds and Nilotic mud.

I thus give the reader some slight abstraction of my oriental dreams, which always filled me with such amazement at the monstrous scenery, that horror seemed absorbed, for a while, in sheer astonishment. Sooner or later, came a reflux of feeling that swallowed up the astonishment, and left me, not so much in terror, as in hatred and abomination of what I saw. Over every form, and threat, and punishment, and dim sightless incarceration, brooded a sense of eternity and infinity that drove me into an oppression as of madness. Into these dreams only, it was, with one or two slight exceptions, that any circumstances of physical horror entered. All before had been moral and spiritual terrors. But here the main agents were ugly birds, or snakes, or crocodiles; especially the last. The cursed crocodile became to me the object of more horror than almost all the rest. I was compelled to live with him; and (as was always the case almost in my dreams) for centuries. I escaped sometimes, and found myself in Chinese houses, with cane tables, &c. All the feet of the tables, sophas, &c. soon became instinct with life: the abominable head of the crocodile, and his leering eyes, looked out at me, multiplied into a thousand repetitions: and I stood loathing and fascinated. And so often did this hideous reptile haunt my dreams, that many times the very same dream was broken up in the very same way: I heard gentle voices speaking to me (I hear everything when I am sleeping); and instantly I awoke: it was broad noon; and my children were standing, hand in hand, at my bed-side; come to show me their coloured shoes, or new frocks, or to let me see them dressed for going out. I protest that so awful was the transition from the damned crocodile, and the unutterable monsters and abortions of my dreams, to the sight of innocent *human natures* and of infancy, that, in the mighty and sudden revulsion of mind, I wept, and could not forbear it, as I kissed their faces.

## 13

## SONG

*Thomas Lovell Beddoes*

Old Adam, the carrion crow,
The old crow of Cairo;
He sat in the shower, and let it flow
Under his tail and over his crest;
And through every feather
Leaked the wet weather;
And the bough swung under his nest;
For his beak it was heavy with marrow.
Is that the wind dying? O no;
It's only two devils, that blow
Through a murderer's bones, to and fro,
In the ghosts' moonshine.

Ho! Eve, my grey carrion wife,
When we have supped on kings' marrow,
Where shall we drink and make merry our life?
Our nest it is queen Cleopatra's skull,
'Tis cloved and cracked,
And battered and hacked,
But with tears of blue eyes it is full:
Let us drink then, my raven of Cairo.
Is that the wind dying? O no;
It's only two devils, that blow
Through a murderer's bones, to and fro,
In the ghosts' moonshine.

## 14

## Verses from LAMIA

*John Keats*

*Part I, 11.47–67*

She was a gordian shape of dazzling hue,
Vermilion-spotted, golden, green, and blue;
Striped like a zebra, freckled like a pard,
Eyed like a peacock, and all crimson barred;
And full of silver moons, that, as she breathed,
Dissolved, or brighter shone, or interwreathed
Their lustres with the gloomier tapestries –
So rainbow-sided, touched with miseries,
She seemed, at once, some penanced lady elf,
Some demon's mistress, or the demon's self.
Upon her crest she wore a fannish fire
Sprinkled with stars, like Ariadne's tiar;
Her head was serpent, but ah, bitter-sweet!
She had a woman's mouth with all its pearls complete;
And for her eyes – what could such eyes do there
But weep, and weep, that they were born so fair,
As Proserpine still weeps for her Sicilian air.
Her throat was serpent, but the words she spake
Came, as through bubbling honey, for Love's sake. . .

## 15

## THOUGHTS DURING SICKNESS
## II. SICKNESS LIKE NIGHT

***Felicia Dorothea Hemans***

Thou art like night, oh sickness, deeply stilling
Within my heart the world's disturbing sound,
And the dim quiet of my chamber filling
With low, sweet voices, by life's tumult drowned.
Thou art like awful night! Thou gatherest round
The things that are unseen, though close they lie,
And with a truth, clear, startling, and profound,
Giv'st their dread presence to our mortal eye.
Thou art like starry, spiritual night!
High and immortal thoughts attend thy way,
And revelations, which the common light
Brings not, though wakening with its rosy ray
All outward life: be welcome, then, thy rod,
Before whose touch my soul unfolds itself to God!

## 16

# TITHONUS

*Alfred, Lord Tennyson*

The woods decay, the woods decay and fall,
The vapours weep their burthen to the ground,
Man comes and tills the field and lies beneath,
And after many a summer dies the swan.
Me only cruel immortality
Consumes: I wither slowly in thine arms,
Here at the quiet limit of the world,
A white-hair'd shadow roaming like a dream
The ever-silent spaces of the East,
Far-folded mists, and gleaming halls of morn.

Alas! for this gray shadow, once a man –
So glorious in his beauty and thy choice,
Who madest him thy chosen, that he seem'd
To his great heart none other than a God!
I ask'd thee, 'Give me immortality.'
Then didst thou grant mine asking with a smile,
Like wealthy men who care not how they give.
But thy strong Hours indignant work'd their wills,
And beat me down and marr'd and wasted me,
And tho' they could not end me, left me maim'd
To dwell in presence of immortal youth,
Immortal age beside immortal youth,
And all I was, in ashes. Can thy love,
Thy beauty, make amends, tho' even now,
Close over us, the silver star, thy guide,
Shines in those tremulous eyes that fill with tears
To hear me? Let me go: take back thy gift:
Why should a man desire in any way
To vary from the kindly race of men,
Or pass beyond the goal of ordinance
Where all should pause, as is most meet for all?

A soft air fans the cloud apart; there comes
A glimpse of that dark world where I was born.
Once more the old mysterious glimmer steals
from thy pure brows, and from thy shoulders pure,
And bosom beating with a heart renew'd.
Thy cheek begins to redden thro' the gloom,
Thy sweet eyes brighten slowly close to mine,
Ere yet they blind the stars, and the wild team
Which love thee, yearning for thy yoke, arise,
And shake the darkness from their loosen'd manes,
And beat the twilight into flakes of fire.

Lo! ever thus thou growest beautiful
In silence, then before thine answer given
Departest, and thy tears are on my cheek.

Why wilt thou ever scare me with thy tears,
And make me tremble lest a saying learnt,
In days far-off, on that dark earth, be true?
'The Gods themselves cannot recall their gifts.'

Ay me! ay me! with what another heart
In days far-off, and with what other eyes
I used to watch – if I be he that watch'd –
The lucid outline forming round thee; saw
The dim curls kindle into sunny rings;
Changed with thy mystic change, and felt my blood
Glow with the glow that slowly crimson'd all
Thy presence and thy portals, while I lay,
Mouth, forehead, eyelids, growing dewy-warm
With kisses balmier than half-opening buds
Of April, and could hear the lips that kiss'd
Whispering I knew not what of wild and sweet,
Like that strange song I heard Apollo sing
While Ilion like a mist rose into towers.

Yet hold me not for ever in thine East:
How can my nature longer mix with thine?

Coldly thy rosy shadows bathe me, cold
Are all thy lights, and cold my wrinkled feet
Upon thy glimmering thresholds, when the steam
Floats up from those dim fields about the homes
Of happy men that have the power to die,
And grassy barrows of the happier dead.
Release me, and restore me to the ground;
Thou seest all things, thou wilt see my grave:
Thou wilt renew thy beauty morn by morn;
I earth in forget these empty courts,
And thee returning on thy silver wheels.

## 17

## BODY'S BEAUTY

***Dante Gabriel Rossetti***

Of Adam's first wife, Lilith, it is told
(The witch he loved before the gift of Eve,)
That, ere the snake's, her sweet tongue could deceive,
And her enchanted hair was the first gold.
And still she sits, young while the earth is old,
And, subtly of herself contemplative,
Draws men to watch the bright web she can weave,
Till heart and body and life are in its hold.

The rose and poppy are her flowers; for where
Is he not found, O Lilith, whom shed scent
And soft-shed kisses and soft sleep shall snare?
Lo! as that youth's eyes burned at thine, so went
Thy spell through him, and left his straight neck bent
And round his heart one strangling golden hair.

## 18

## Verses from ANACTORIA

*Algernon Charles Swinburne*

ll. 1–58

My life is bitter with thy love; thine eyes
Blind me, thy tresses burn me, thy sharp sighs
Divide my flesh and spirit with soft sound,
And my blood strengthens, and my veins abound.
I pray thee sigh not, speak not, draw not breath;
Let life burn down, and dream it is not death.
I would the sea had hidden us, the fire
(Wilt thou fear that, and fear not my desire?)
Severed the bones that bleach, the flesh that cleaves
And let our sifted ashes drop like leaves.
I feel thy blood against my blood: my pain
Pains thee, and lips bruise lips, and vein stings vein.
Let fruit be crushed on fruit, let flower on flower,
Breast kindle breast, and either burn one hour.
Why wilt thou follow lesser loves? are thine
Too weak to bear these hands and lips of mine?
I charge thee for my life's sake, O too sweet
To crush love with thy cruel faultless feet,
I charge thee keep thy lips from hers or his,
Sweetest, till theirs be sweeter than my kiss:
Lest I too lure, a swallow for a dove,
Erotion or Erinna to my love.
I would my love could kill thee; I am satiated
With seeing thee live, and fain would have thee dead.
I would earth had thy body as fruit to eat,
And no mouth but some serpent's found thee sweet.
I would find grievous ways to have thee slain,
Intense device, and superflux of pain;
Vex thee with amorous agonies, and shake

Life at thy lips, and leave it there to ache;
Strain out thy soul with pangs too soft to kill,
Intolerable interludes, and infinite ill;
Relapse and reluctation of the breath,
Dumb tunes and shuddering semitones of death.
I am weary of all thy words and soft strange ways,
Of all love's fiery nights and all his days,
And all the broken kisses salt as brine
That shuddering lips make moist with waterish wine,
And eyes the bluer for all those hidden hours
That pleasure fills with tears and feeds from flowers,
Fierce at the heart with fire that half comes through,
But all the flowerlike white stained round with blue
The fervent underlid, and that above
Lifted with laughter or abashed with love;
Thine amorous girdle, full of thee and fair,
And leavings of the lilies in thine hair.
Yea, all sweet words of thine and all thy ways,
And all the fruit of nights and flower of days,
And stinging lips wherein the hot sweet brine
That Love was born of burns and foams like wine,
And eyes insatiable of amorous hours,
Fervent as fire and delicate as flowers,
Coloured like night at heart, but cloven through
Like night with flame, dyed round like night with blue
Clothed with deep eyelids under and above –
Yea, all thy beauty sickens me with love;
Thy girdle empty of thee and now not fair,
And ruinous lilies in thy languid hair.

## 19

# Extract from STUDIES IN THE HISTORY OF THE RENAISSANCE

***Walter Pater***

from the Conclusion

*'Heraclitus says "All things give way: nothing remaineth" '*

. . . At first sight experience seems to bury us under a flood of external objects, pressing upon us with a sharp and importunate reality, calling us out of ourselves in a thousand forms of action. But when reflexion begins to play upon those objects they are dissipated under its influence; the cohesive force seems suspended like some trick of magic; each object is loosed into a group of impressions – colour, odour, texture – in the mind of the observer. And if we continue to dwell in thought on this world, not of objects in the solidity with which language invests them, but of impressions, unstable, flickering, inconsistent, which burn and are extinguished with our consciousness of them, it contracts still further: the whole scope of observation is dwarfed into the narrow chamber of the individual mind. Experience, already reduced to a group of impressions, is ringed round for each one of us by that thick wall of personality through which no real voice has ever pierced on its way to us, or from us to that which we can only conjecture to be without. Every one of those impressions is the impression of the individual in his isolation, each mind keeping as a solitary prisoner its own dream of a world. Analysis goes a step further still, and assures us that those impressions of the individual mind to which, for each one of us, experience dwindles down, are in perpetual flight; that each of them is limited by time, and that as time is infinitely divisible, each of them is infinitely divisible also; all that is actual in it being a single moment, gone while we try to apprehend it, of which it may ever be more truly said that it has ceased to be than that it is. To such a tremulous wisp constantly re-forming itself on the stream, to a single sharp impression, with a sense in it, a relic more or less fleeting, of such moments gone by, what is real in our life fines itself down. It is with this movement, with the passage and dissolution of impressions, images, sensations, that analysis leaves off – that continual vanishing away, that strange, perpetual, weaving and unweaving of ourselves.

*Philosophiren*, says Novalis, *ist dephlegmatisiren, vivificiren*. The service of philosophy, of speculative culture, towards the human spirit, is to rouse, to startle it to a life of constant and eager observation. Every moment some form grows perfect in hand or face; some tone on the hills or the sea is choicer than the rest; some mood of passion or insight or intellectual excitement is irresistibly real and attractive to us, – for that moment only. Not the fruit of experience, but experience itself, is the end. A counted number of pulses only is given to us of a variegated, dramatic life. How may we see in them all that is to be seen in them by the finest senses? How shall we pass most swiftly from point to point, and be present always at the focus where the greatest number of vital forces unite in their present energy?

To burn always with this hard, gem-like flame, to maintain this ecstasy, is success in life. In a sense it might even be said that our failure is to form habits: for, after all, habit is relative to a stereotyped world, and meantime it is only the roughness of the eye that makes any two persons, things, situations, seem alike. While all melts under our feet, we may well grasp at any exquisite passion, or any contribution to knowledge that seems by a lifted horizon to set the spirit free for a moment, or any stirring of the senses, strange dyes, strange colours, and curious odours, or work of the artist's hands, or the face of one's friend. Not to discriminate every moment some passionate attitude in those about us, and in the very brilliancy of their gifts some tragic dividing of forces on their ways, is, on this short day of frost and sun, to sleep before evening. With this sense of the splendour of our experience and of its awful brevity, gathering all we are into one desperate effort to see and touch, we shall hardly have time to make theories about the things we see and touch. What we have to do is to be for ever curiously testing new opinions and courting new impressions, never acquiescing in a facile orthodoxy, of Comte, or of Hegel, or of our own. Philosophical theories or ideas, as points of view, instruments of criticism, may help us to gather up what might otherwise pass unregarded by us. 'Philosophy is the microscope of thought.' The theory or idea or system which requires of us the sacrifice of any part of this experience, in consideration of some interest into which we cannot enter, or some abstract theory we have not identified with ourselves, or of what is only unconventional, has no real claim upon us.

One of the most beautiful passages of Rousseau is that in the sixth book of the *Confessions*, where he describes the awakening in him of the literary sense. An undefinable taint of death had always clung about him, and now in early manhood he believed himself smitten by mortal disease. He asked himself how he might make as much as possible of the interval that remained; and he was not biased by anything in his previous life when he decided that it must be by intellectual excitement, which he found just then in the clear, fresh writings of Voltaire. Well! we are all *condamnés*, as Victor Hugo says: we are all under sentence of death but with a sort of indefinite reprieve – *les hommes sont tous condamnés à mort avec des sursis indéfinis* : we have an interval, and then our place knows us no more. Some spend this interval in listlessness, some in high passions, the wisest, at least among 'the children of this world', in art and song. For our one chance lies in expanding that interval, in getting as many pulsations as possible into the given time. Great passions may give us this quickened sense of life, ecstasy and sorrow of love, the various forms of enthusiastic activity, disinterested or otherwise, which come naturally to many of us. Only be sure it is passion – that it does yield you this fruit of a quickened, multiplied consciousness. Of such wisdom, the poetic passion, the desire of beauty, the love of art for its own sake, has most. For art comes to you proposing frankly to give nothing but the highest quality to your moments as they pass, and simply for those moments' sake.

## 20

## IF YOU'RE ANXIOUS FOR TO SHINE IN THE HIGH AESTHETIC LINE from PATIENCE

***Sir W. S. Gilbert***

Am I alone,
And unobserved? I am!

Then let me own
I'm an aesthetic sham!

This air severe
Is but a mere
Veneer!

This cynic smile
Is but a wile
Of guile!
This costume chaste

Is but good taste
Misplaced!

Let me confess!
A languid love for lilies does *not* blight me!
Lank limbs and haggard cheeks do *not* delight me!
I do *not* care for dirty greens
By any means.
I do *not* long for all one sees
That's Japanese.
I am *not* fond of uttering platitudes
In stained-glass attitudes.
In short, my medievalism's affectation,
Born of a morbid love of admiration!

If you're anxious for to shine in the high aesthetic line as
a man of culture rare,

You must get up all the germs of the transcendental terms, and plant them everywhere.
You must lie upon the daisies and discourse in novel phrases of your complicated state of mind,
The meaning doesn't matter if it's only idle chatter of a transcendental kind.

And everyone will say,
As you walk your mystic way,

'If this young man expresses himself in terms too deep for *me*,
Why, what a very singularly deep young man this deep young man must be!'

Be eloquent in praise of the very dull old days which have long since passed away,
And convince 'em, if you can, that the reign of good Queen Anne was Culture's palmiest day.
Of course you will pooh-pooh whatever's fresh and new, and declare it's crude and mean,
For Art stopped short in the cultivated court of the Empress Josephine.

And everyone will say,
As you walk your mystic way,

'If that's not good enough for him which is good enough for *me*,
Why, what a very cultivated kind of youth this kind of youth must be!'

Then a sentimental passion of a vegetable fashion must excite your languid spleen,
An attachment *à la* Plato for a bashful young potato, or a not-too-French French bean!
Though the Philistines may jostle, you will rank as an apostle in the high aesthetic band,

If you walk down Piccadilly with a poppy or a lily in
your medieval hand.

And everyone will say,
As you walk your flowery way,

'If he's content with a vegetable love which would
certainly not suit *me*,
Why, what a most particularly pure young man this pure
young man must be!'

## 21

## DOLORES
## (NOTRE DAME DES SEPT DOULEURS)
### *Algernon Charles Swinburne*

Cold eyelids that hide like a jewel
　Hard eyes that grow soft for an hour;
The heavy white limbs, and the cruel
　Red mouth like a venomous flower;
When these are gone by with their glories,
　What shall rest of thee then, what shall remain,
O mystic and sombre Dolores,
　Our Lady of Pain?

Seven sorrows the priests give their Virgin;
　But thy sins, which are seventy times seven,
Seven ages would fail thee to purge in,
　And then they would haunt thee in heaven:
Fierce midnights and famishing morrows,
　And the loves that complete and control
All the joys of the flesh, all the sorrows
　That wear out the soul.

O garment not golden but gilded,
　O garden where all men may dwell,
O tower not of ivory, but builded
　By hands that reach heaven from hell;
O mystical rose of the mire,
　O house not of gold but of gain,
O house of unquenchable fire,
　Our Lady of Pain!

O lips full of lust and laughter,
　Curled snakes that are fed from my breast,
Bite hard, lest remembrance come after
　And press with new lips where you pressed.

For my heart too springs up at the pressure,
   Mine eyelids too moisten and burn;
Ah, feed me and fill me with pleasure,
   Ere pain come in turn.

In yesterday's reach and tomorrow's,
   Out of sight though they lie of to-day,
There have been and there yet shall be sorrows
   That smite not and bite not in play.
The life and the love thou despisest,
   These hurt us indeed, and in vain,
O wise among women, and wisest,
   Our Lady of Pain.

Who gave thee thy wisdom? what stories
   That stung thee, what visions that smote?
Wert thou pure and a maiden, Dolores,
   When desire took thee first by the throat?
What bud was the shell of a blossom
   That all men may smell to and pluck?
What milk fed thee first at what bosom?
   What sins gave thee suck?

We shift and bedeck and bedrape us,
   Thou art noble and nude and antique;
Libitina thy mother, Priapus
   Thy father, a Tuscan and a Greek.
We play with light loves in the portal,
   And wince and relent and refrain;
Loves die, and we know thee immortal,
   Our Lady of Pain.

Fruits fail and love dies and time ranges;
   Thou art fed with perpetual breath,
And alive after infinite changes,
   And fresh from the kisses of death;
Of languors rekindled and rallied,
   Of barren delights and unclean,

Things monstrous and fruitless, a pallid
  And poisonous queen.

Could you hurt me, sweet lips, though I hurt you?
  Men touch them, and change in a trice
The lilies and languors of virtue
  For the raptures and roses of vice;
Those lie where thy foot on the floor is,
  These crown and caress thee and chain,
O splendid and sterile Dolores,
  Our Lady of Pain.

There are sins it may be to discover,
  There are deeds it may be to delight.
What new work wilt thou find for thy lover,
  What new passions for daytime or night?
What spells that they know not a word of
  Whose lives are as leaves overblown?
What tortures undreamt of, unheard of,
  Unwritten, unknown?

Ah beautiful passionate body
  That never has ached with a heart!
On thy mouth though the kisses are bloody,
  Though they sting till it shudder and smart,
More kind than the love we adore is,
  They hurt not the heart or the brain,
O bitter and tender Dolores,
  Our Lady of Pain.

As our kisses relax and redouble,
  From the lips and the foam and the fangs
Shall no new sin be born for men's trouble,
  No dream of impossible pangs?
With the sweet of the sins of old ages
  Wilt thou satiate thy soul as of yore?
Too sweet is the rind, say the sages,
  Too bitter the core.

Hast thou told all thy secrets the last time,
  And bared all thy beauties to one?
Ah, where shall we go then for pastime,
  If the worst that can be has been done?
But sweet as the rind was the core is;
  We are fain of thee still, we are fain,
O sanguine and subtle Dolores,
  Our Lady of Pain.

By the hunger of change and emotion,
  By the thirst of unbearable things,
By despair, the twin-born of devotion,
  By the pleasure that winces and stings,
The delight that consumes the desire,
  The desire that outruns the delight,
By the cruelty deaf as a fire
  And blind as the night,

By the ravenous teeth that have smitten
  Through the kisses that blossom and bud,
By the lips intertwisted and bitten
  Till the foam has a savour of blood,
By the pulse as it rises and falters,
  By the hands as they slacken and strain,
I adjure thee, respond from thine altars,
  Our Lady of Pain.

Wilt thou smile as a woman disdaining
  The light fire in the veins of a boy?
But he who comes to thee sad, without feigning,
  Who has wearied of sorrow and joy;
Less careful of labour and glory
  Than the elders whose hair has uncurled;
And young, but with fancies as hoary
  And grey as the world.

I have passed from the outermost portal
  To the shrine where the sin is a prayer;

What care though the service be mortal?
O our Lady of Torture, what care?
All thine the last wine that I pour is,
The last in the chalice we drain,
O fierce and luxurious Dolores,
Our Lady of Pain.

All thine the new wine of desire,
The fruit of four lips as they clung
Till the hair and the eyelids took fire,
The foam of a serpentine tongue,
The froth of the serpents of pleasure,
More salt than the foam of the sea,
Now felt as a flame, now at leisure
As wine shed for me.

Ah thy people, thy children, thy chosen,
Marked cross from the womb and perverse!
They have found out the secret to cozen
The gods that constrain us and curse;
They alone, they are wise, and none other;
Give me place, even me, in their train,
O my sister, my spouse, and my mother,
Our Lady of Pain.

For the crown of our life as it closes
Is darkness, the fruit thereof dust;
No thorns go as deep as a rose's,
And love is more cruel than lust.
Time turns the old days to derision,
Our loves into corpses or wives;
And marriage and death and division
Make barren our lives.

And pale from the past we draw nigh thee,
And satiate with comfortless hours;
And we know thee, how all men belie thee,
And we gather the fruit of thy flowers;

The passion that slays and recovers,
  The pangs and the kisses that rain
On the lips and the limbs of thy lovers,
  Our Lady of Pain.

The desire of thy furious embraces
  Is more than the wisdom of years,
On the blossom though the blood lie in traces,
  Though the foliage be sodden with tears.
For the lords in whose keeping the door is
  That opens on all who draw breath
Gave the cypress to love, my Dolores,
  The myrtle to death.

And they laughed, changing hands in the measure.
  And they mixed and made peace after strife;
Pain melted in tears, and was pleasure;
  Death tingled with blood, and was life.
Like lovers they melted and tingled,
  In the dusk of thine innermost fane;
In the darkness they murmured and mingled,
  Our Lady of Pain.

In a twilight where virtues are vices,
  In thy chapels, unknown of the sun,
To a tune that enthralls and entices,
  They are wed, and the twain were as one.
For the tune from thine altar hath sounded
  Since God bade the world's work begin,
And the fume of thine incense abounded,
  To sweeten the sin.

Love listens, and paler than ashes,
  Through his curls as the crown on them slips,
Lifts languid wet eyelids and lashes,
  And laughs with insatiable lips.
Thou shalt hush him with heavy caresses,
  With music that scares the profane;

Thou shalt darken his eyes with thy tresses,
   Our Lady of Pain.

Thou shalt blind his bright eyes though he wrestle,
   Thou shalt chain his light limbs though he strive;
In his lips all thy servants shall nestle,
   In his hands all thy cruelties thrive.
In the daytime thy voice shall go through him,
   In his dreams he shall feel thee and ache;
Thou shalt kindle by night and subdue him
   Asleep and awake.

Thou shalt touch and make redder his roses
   With juice not of fruit nor of bud;
When the sense in the spirit reposes,
   Thou shalt quicken the soul through the blood.
Thine, thine the one grace we implore is,
   Who would live and not languish or feign,
O sleepless and deadly Dolores,
   Our Lady of Pain.

Dost thou dream, in a respite of slumber,
   In a lull of the fires of thy life,
Of the days without name, without number,
   When thy will stung the world into strife;
When, a goddess, the pulse of thy passion
   Smote kings as they revelled in Rome;
And they hailed thee re-risen, O Thalassian,
   Foam-white, from the foam?

When thy lips had such lovers to flatter;
   When the city lay red from thy rods,
And thine hands were as arrows to scatter
   The children of change and their gods;
When the blood of thy foemen made fervent
   A sand never moist from the main,
As one smote them, their lord and thy servant,
   Our Lady of Pain.

On sands by the storm never shaken,
   Nor wet from the washing of tides;
Nor by foam of the waves overtaken,
   Nor winds that the thunder bestrides;
But red from the print of thy paces,
   Made smooth for the world and its lords,
Ringed round with a ring of fair faces,
   And splendid with swords.

There the gladiator, pale for thy pleasure,
   Drew bitter and perilous breath;
There torments lay hold on the treasure
   Of limbs too delicious for death;
When thy gardens were lit with live torches;
   When the world was a steed for thy rein;
When the nations lay prone in their porches,
   Our Lady of Pain.

When, with flame all around him aspirant,
   Stood flushed, as a harp-player stands,
The implacable beautiful tyrant,
   Rose-crowned, having death in his hands;
And a sound as the sound of loud water
   Smote far through the flight of the fires,
And mixed with the lightning of slaughter
   A thunder of lyres.

Dost thou dream of what was and no more is.
   The old kingdoms of earth and the kings?
Dost thou hunger for these things, Dolores,
   For these, in a world of new things?
But thy bosom no fasts could emaciate,
   No hunger compel to complain
Those lips that no bloodshed could satiate,
   Our Lady of Pain.

As of old when the world's heart was lighter,
   Through thy garments the grace of thee glows,

The white wealth of thy body made whiter
  By the blushes of amorous blows,
And seamed with sharp lips and fierce fingers,
  And branded by kisses that bruise;
When all shall be gone that now lingers,
  Ah, what shall we lose?

Thou wert fair in the fearless old fashion,
  And thy limbs are as melodies yet,
And move to the music of passion
  With lithe and lascivious regret.
What ailed us, O gods, to desert you
  For creeds that refuse and restrain?
Come down and redeem us from virtue,
  Our Lady of Pain.

All shrines that were Vestal are flameless,
  But the flame has not fallen from this;
Though obscure be the god, and though nameless
  The eyes and the hair that we kiss;
Low fires that love sits by and forges
  Fresh heads for his arrows and thine;
Hair loosened and soiled in mid orgies
  With kisses and wine.

Thy skin changes country and colour,
  And shrivels or swells to a snakes'.
Let it brighten and bloat and grow duller,
  We know it, the flames and the flakes,
Red brands on it smitten and bitten,
  Round skies where a star is a stain,
And the leaves with thy litanies written,
  Our Lady of Pain.

On thy bosom though many a kiss be,
  There are none such as knew it of old.
Was it Alciphron once or Arisbe,
  Male ringlets or feminine gold,

That thy lips met with under the statue,
  Whence a look shot out sharp after thieves
From the eyes of the garden-god at you
  Across the fig-leaves?

Then still, through dry seasons and moister,
  One god had a wreath to his shrine;
Then love was the pearl of his oyster,
  And Venus rose red out of wine.
We have all done amiss, choosing rather
  Such loves as the wise gods disdain;
Intercede for us thou with thy father,
  Our Lady of Pain.

In spring he had crowns of his garden,
  Red corn in the heat of the year,
Then hoary green olives that harden
  When the grape-blossom freezes with fear;
And milk-budded myrtles with Venus
  And vine-leaves with Bacchus he trod;
And ye said, 'We have seen, he hath seen us,
  A visible God.'

What broke off the garlands that girt you?
  What sundered you spirit and clay?
Weak sins yet alive are as virtue
  To the strength of the sins of that day.
For dried is the blood of thy lover,
  Ipsithilla, contracted the vein;
Cry aloud, 'Will he rise and recover,
  Our Lady of Pain?'

Cry aloud; for the old world is broken:
  Cry out; for the Phrygian is priest,
And rears not the bountiful token
  And spreads not the fatherly feast.
From the midmost of Ida, from shady
  Recesses that murmur at morn,

They have brought and baptized her, Our Lady,
   A goddess new-born.

And the chaplets of old are above us,
   And the oyster-bed teems out of reach;
Old poets outsing and outlove us,
   And Catullus makes mouths at our speech.
Who shall kiss, in thy father's own city,
   With such lips as he sang with, again?
Intercede for us all of thy pity,
   Our Lady of Pain.

Out of Dindymus heavily laden
   Her lions draw bound and unfed
A mother, a mortal, a maiden,
   A queen over death and the dead.
She is cold, and her habit is lowly,
   Her temple of branches and sods;
Most fruitful and virginal, holy,
   A mother of gods.

She hath wasted with fire thine high places,
   She hath hidden and marred and made sad
The fair limbs of the Loves, the fair faces
   Of gods that were goodly and glad.
She slays, and her hands are not bloody;
   She moves as a moon in the wane,
White-robed, and thy raiment is ruddy,
   Our Lady of Pain.

They shall pass and their places be taken,
   The gods and the priests that are pure.
They shall pass, and shalt thou not be shaken?
   They shall perish, and shalt thou not endure?
Death laughs, breathing close and relentless
   In the nostrils and eyelids of lust,
With a pinch in his fingers of scentless
   And delicate dust.

But the worm shall revive thee with kisses;
  Thou shalt change and transmute as a god,
As the rod to a serpent that hisses,
  As the serpent again to a rod.
Thy life shall not cease though thou doff it;
  Thou shalt live until evil be slain,
And good shall die first, said thy prophet,
  Our Lady of Pain.

Did he lie? did he laugh? does he know it,
  Now he lies out of reach, out of breath,
Thy prophet, thy preacher, thy poet,
  Sin's child by incestuous Death?
Did he find out in fire at his waking,
  Or discern as his eyelids lost light,
When the bands of the body were breaking
  And all came in sight?

Who has known all the evil before us,
  Or the tyrannous secrets of time?
Though we match not the dead men that bore us
  At a song, at a kiss, at a crime –
Though the heathen outface and outlive us,
  And our lives and our longings are twain –
Ah, forgive us our virtues, forgive us,
  Our Lady of Pain.

Who are we that embalm and embrace thee
  With spices and savours of song?
What is time, that his children should face thee?
  What am I, that my lips do thee wrong?
I could hurt thee – but pain would delight thee;
  Or caress thee – but love would repel;
And the lovers whose lips would excite thee
  Are serpents in hell.

Who now shall content thee as they did,
  Thy lovers, when temples were built

And the hair of the sacrifice braided
And the blood of the sacrifice spilt,
In Lampsacus fervent with faces,
In Aphaca red from thy reign,
Who embraced thee with awful embraces,
Our Lady of Pain?

Where are they, Cotytto or Venus,
Astarte or Ashtaroth, where?
Do their hands as we touch come between us?
Is the breath in them hot in thy hair?
From their lips have thy lips taken fever,
With the blood of their bodies grown red?
Hast thou left upon earth a believer
If these men are dead?

They were purple of raiment and golden,
Filled full of thee, fiery with wine,
Thy lovers, in haunts unbeholden,
In marvellous chambers of thine.
They are fled, and their footprints escape us,
Who appraise thee, adore, and abstain,
O daughter of death and Priapus,
Our Lady of Pain.

What ails us to fear overmeasure,
To praise thee with timorous breath,
O mistress and mother of pleasure,
The one thing as certain as death?
We shall change as the things that we cherish,
Shall fade as they faded before,
As foam upon water shall perish,
As sand upon shore.

We shall know what the darkness discovers,
If the grave-pit be shallow or deep;
And our fathers of old, and our lovers,
We shall know if they sleep not or sleep.

We shall see whether hell not be heaven,
  Find out whether tares not be grain,
And the joys of thee seventy times seven,
  Our Lady of Pain.

## 22

## HÉLAS!

*Oscar Wilde*

To drift with every passion till my soul
Is a stringed lute on which all winds can play,
Is it for this that I have given away
Mine ancient wisdom, and austere control?
Methinks my life is a twice-written scroll
Scrawled over on some boyish holiday
With idle songs for pipe and virelay,
Which do but mar the secret of the whole.
Surely there was a time I might have trod
The sunlit heights, and from life's dissonance
Struck one clear chord to reach the ears of God:
Is that time dead? Lo! with a little rod
I did but touch the honey of romance –
And must I lose a soul's inheritance?

# 23

## Passages from
## CONFESSIONS OF A YOUNG MAN
### *George Moore*

from Chapter I

My soul, so far as I understand it, has very kindly taken colour and form from the many various modes of life that self-will and an impetuous temperament have forced me to indulge in. Therefore I may say that I am free from original qualities, defects, tastes, etc. What is mine I have acquired, or, to speak more exactly, chance bestowed, and still bestows, upon me. I came into the world apparently with a nature like a smooth sheet of wax, bearing no impress, but capable of receiving any; of being moulded into all shapes. Nor am I exaggerating when I say I think that I might equally have been a Pharaoh, an ostler, a pimp, an archbishop, and that in the fulfilment of the duties of each a certain measure of success would have been mine. I have felt the goad of many impulses, I have hunted many a trail; when one scent failed another was taken up, and pursued with the pertinacity of instinct, rather than the fervour of a reasoned conviction. Sometimes, it is true, there came moments of weariness, of despondency, but they were not enduring: a word spoken, a book read, or yielding to the attraction of environment, I was soon off in another direction, forgetful of past failures. Intricate, indeed, was the labyrinth of my desires; all lights were followed with the same ardour, all cries were eagerly responded to: they came from the right, they came from the left, from every side. But one cry was more persistent, and as the years passed I learned to follow it with increasing vigour, and my strayings grew fewer and the way wider.

★ ★ ★ ★ ★ ★ ★ ★ ★ ★ ★ ★

from Chapter IX

Pity, that most vile of all virtues, has never been known to me. The great pagan world I love knew it not. Now the world proposes to interrupt the terrible austere laws of nature which ordain that the weak shall be trampled upon, shall be ground into death and dust, that the strong shall be really strong – that the strong shall be glorious, sublime. A little bourgeois comfort, a little bourgeois sense of right, cry the moderns.

Hither the world has been drifting since the coming of the pale socialist of Galilee; and this is why I hate Him, and deny His divinity. His divinity is falling, it is evanescent in sight of the goal He dreamed; again He is denied by his disciples. Poor fallen God! I, who hold naught else pitiful, pity Thee, Thy bleeding face and hands and feet, Thy hanging body; Thou at least art picturesque, and in a way beautiful in the midst of the sombre mediocrity, towards which Thou hast drifted for two thousand years, a flag; and in which Thou shalt find Thy doom as I mine, I, who will not adore Thee and cannot curse Thee now. For verily Thy life and Thy fate has been greater, stranger and more Divine than any man's has been. The chosen people, the garden, the betrayal, the crucifixion, and the beautiful story, not of Mary, but of Magdalen. The God descending to the Magdalen! Even the great pagan world of marble and pomp and lust and cruelty, that my soul goes out to and hails as the grandest, has not so sublime a contrast to show us as this.

Come to me, ye who are weak. The Word went forth, the terrible disastrous Word, and before it fell the ancient gods, and the vices that they represent, and which I revere, are outcast now in the world of men; the Word went forth, and the world interpreted the Word, blindly, ignorantly, savagely, for two thousand years, but nevertheless nearing every day the end – the end that Thou in Thy divine intelligence foresawest, that finds its voice to-day (enormous though the antithesis may be, I will say it) in the *Pall Mall Gazette*. What fate has been like Thine? Betrayed by Judas in the garden, denied by Peter before the cock crew, crucified between thieves, and mourned for by a Magdalen, and then sent bound and bare, nothing changed, nothing altered, in Thy ignominious plight, forthward in the world's van the glory and symbol of man's new idea – Pity. Thy day is closing in, but the heavens are now wider aflame with Thy light than ever before – Thy light, which I, a pagan, standing on the last verge of the old world, declare to be darkness, the coming night of pity and justice which is imminent, which is the twentieth century. The bearers have relinquished Thy cross, they leave Thee in the hour of Thy universal triumph, Thy crown of thorns is falling, Thy face is buffeted with blows, and not even a reed is placed in Thy hand for sceptre; only I and mine are by Thee, we who shall perish with Thee, in the ruin Thou hast created.

Injustice we worship; all that lifts us out of the miseries of life is the sublime fruit of injustice. Every immortal deed was an act of fearful injustice; the world of grandeur, of triumph, of courage, of lofty aspiration, was built up on injustice. Man would not be man but for injustice. Hail, therefore, to the thrice glorious virtue injustice! What care I that some millions of wretched Israelites died under Pharaoh's lash or Egypt's sun? It was well that they died that I might have the pyramids to look on, or to fill a musing hour with wonderment. Is there one amongst us who would exchange them for the lives of the ignominious slaves that died? What care I that the virtue of some sixteen-year-old maiden was the price paid for Ingres' 'La Source'? That the model died of drink and disease in the hospital, is nothing when compared with the essential that I should have 'La Source,' that exquisite dream of innocence, to think of till my soul is sick with delight of the painter's holy vision. Nay more, the knowledge that a wrong was done – that millions of Israelites died in torments, that a girl, or a thousand girls, died in the hospital for that one virginal thing, is an added pleasure which I could not afford to spare. Oh, for the silence of marble courts, for the shadow of great pillars, for gold, for recapitulated canopies of lilies; to see the great gladiators pass, to hear them cry the infamous, 'Ave Caesar,' to hold the thumb down, to see the blood flow, to fill the languid hours with the agonies of poisoned slaves! Oh, for excess, for crime! I would give many lives to save one sonnet by Baudelaire; for the hymn, '*À la très chère, à la très belle, qui remplit mon cœur de clarté,*' let the first-born in every house in Europe be slain; and in all sincerity I profess my readiness to decapitate all the Japanese in Japan and elsewhere, to save from destruction one drawing by Hokusai. Again I say that all we deem sublime in the world's history are acts of injustice; and it is certain that if mankind does not relinquish at once, and for ever, its vain, mad, and fatal dream of justice, the world will lapse into barbarism. England was great and glorious, because England was unjust, and England's greatest son was the personification of injustice – Cromwell.

## 24

## NIGHTMARE from THE CITY OF DREADFUL NIGHT

***James Thomson***

As I came through the desert thus it was,
As I came through the desert: All was black,
In heaven no single star, on earth no track;
A brooding hush without a stir or note,
The air so thick it clotted in my throat;
And thus for hours; then some enormous things
Swooped past with savage cries and clanking wings:
   But I strode on austere;
   No hope could have no fear.

As I came through the desert, thus it was,
As I came through the desert: Eyes of fire
Glared at me throbbing with a starved desire;
The hoarse and heavy and carnivorous breath
Was hot upon me from deep jaws of death;
Sharp claws, swift talons, fleshless fingers cold
Plucked at me from the bushes, tried to hold:
   But I strode on austere;
   No hope could have no fear.

As I came through the desert thus it was,
As I came through the desert: Meteors ran
And crossed their javelins on the black sky-span;
The zenith opened to a gulf of flame,
The dreadful thunderbolts jarred earth's fixed frame:
The ground all heaved in waves of fire that surged
And weltered round me sole there unsubmerged:
   Yet I strode on austere;
   No hope could have no fear.

As I came through the desert thus it was,
As I came through the desert: Air once more,
And I was close upon a wild sea-shore;
Enormous cliffs arose at either hand,
The deep tide thundered up a league-broad strand;
White foam-belts seethed there, wan spray swept and
flew;
The sky broke, moon and stars and clouds and blue:
And I strode on austere:
No hope could have no fear.

As I came through the desert thus it was,
As I came through the desert: From the right
A shape came slowly with a ruddy light;
A woman with a red lamp in her hand,
Bareheaded and barefooted on that strand;
O desolation moving with such grace!
O anguish with such beauty in thy face.
I fell as on my bier,
Hope travailed with such fear.

As I came through the desert thus it was,
As I came through the desert: I was twain,
Two selves distinct that cannot join again;
One stood apart and knew but could not stir,
And watched the other stark in swoon and her;
And she came on, and never turned aside,
Between such sun and moon and roaring tide:
And as she came more near
My soul grew mad with fear.

⋆ ⋆ ⋆ ⋆ ⋆ ⋆ ⋆ ⋆ ⋆ ⋆ ⋆ ⋆

As I came through the desert thus it was,
As I came through the desert: When the tide
Swept up to her there kneeling by my side,
She clasped that corpse-like me, and they were borne
Away, and this vile me was left forlorn;
I know the whole sea cannot quench that heart,

Or cleanse that brow, or wash those two apart:
They love; their doom is drear,
Yet they nor hope nor fear;
But I, what do I here?

## 25

## Passages from *LESBIA BRANDON* *Algernon Charles Swinburne*

from Chapter XVI

He had never come near the dead or dying since his tenth year, when his father died at Kirklowes: but he knew there was a savour of death in the room: something beyond the sweet strong smell of perfumes and drugs. The woman's sad and slow suicide had been with time and care duly accomplished. She had killed herself off by inches, with the help of eau-de-cologne and doses of opium. A funereal fragrance hung about all the air. Close curtains shut out the twilight, and a covered lamp at either end filled the room with less of light than of silver shadow. Along her sofa, propped by cushions and with limbs drawn up like a tired child's, lay or leant a woman like a ghost; the living corpse of Lesbia. She was white, with grey lips; her long shapely hands were pale and faded, and the dark tender warmth of her even colour had changed into a hot and haggard hue like fever. Her beauty of form was unimpaired; she retained the distinction of noble and graceful features and attitudes. She looked like one whom death was as visibly devouring limb-meal as though fire had caught hold of her bound at a stake: like one whose life had been long sapped and undermined from the roots by some quiet fiery poison. Her eyes and hair alone had a look of life: they were brilliant and soft yet, as she reached out her worn hot hands. Herbert came to her with a sense of pressure at his heart, and something like horror and fear mixed with the bitterness of natural pain. The figure and the place were lurid in his eyes, and less fit to make one weep than to make him kindle and tremble. There was an attraction in them which shot heat into his veins instead of the chill and heaviness of terror or grief.

★ ★ ★ ★ ★ ★ ★ ★ ★ ★ ★ ★

She stretched out her weary arms, and lifted herself from heel to shoulder, and with a great sigh, bending her body like a bow, so that for a minute only the head and feet had any support: then slowly relaxed her lifted limbs, and relapsed into supine and sad prostration.

'I dreamt of the old stories; I was always fond of them. I saw Lethe; it was not dark water, nor slow. It was pale and rapid and steady; there was a smell of meadowsweet on the banks. I must have been thinking of your Ensdon woods. And when one came close there was a new smell, more faint and rank; it came from the water-flowers; many were dead and decaying, and all sickly. And opposite me just across there ran out a wharf into the water: like the end of the pier at Wansdale. I saw nothing anywhere that was not like something I had seen already. I can't get that out of my head; as soon as I woke it frightened me: but I didn't wake at once. I remember the green ooze and slime on the piles of the wharf; it was all matted with dead soft stuff that smelt wet. Not like the smell of the sea, but the smell of a lock in the river. And no boat came, and I didn't want one. I felt growing deliciously cold inside my head and behind my eyelids and down to the palms of my hands and feet. I ought to have awaked with a sneeze, and found I had caught cold in fact: but I didn't. And I saw no face anywhere for hours; and that was like a beginning of rest. Then I tried to see Proserpine, and saw her. She stood up to the knees almost in full-blown poppies, single and double. She was not the old Proserpine who comes and goes up and down between Sicily and hell; she had never seen the sun. She was pale and pleased; there was nothing in her like memory or aspiration. The dead element was vital for her; she could not have breathed in higher or lower air. The poppies at her foot were red, and those in her hand were white.'

'Well?' said Herbert as she paused: her voice had filled him with subtle dim emotions, and he was absorbed at once by the strange sound and sense of the words.

'She had grey eyes, bluish like the mingling of mist and water; and soft hair that lay about her breast and arms in sharp pointed locks like tongues of fire. As she looked at me this hair began to vibrate with the sudden motion of her breast, and her eyes brightened into the brilliance of eyes I knew; your sister's; and I began to wonder if she would melt entirely into that likeness. All the time I knew it was impossible she should, because she was incarnate death; and the other I knew was alive. And behind her the whole place all at once became populous with pale figures, hollow all through like an empty dress set upright; stately shadows with a grey light reflected against them; and the whole world as far as I saw was not in darkness, but under a solid cloud that never moved and made the air darker and cooler than the mistiest day upon earth. And in the fields beyond the water there was a splendid harvest of aconite: no other flower anywhere; but the grass was as pale, all yellow and brown, as if the sun had burnt it. Only where the goddess stood there were poppies growing apart; and their red cups, and the big blue lamps of the aconite, all alike hung heavily without wind. I remember, when I was little, wondering whether those flowers were likest lamps or bells; I thought any light or sound that could come of them must be so like the daylight and the music of a dead world. Well, I don't remember much more: but I was haunted with the fear that there might be nothing new behind death after all; no real rest and no real change. And the flowers vexed me. Only these, and no roses; I thought that white single sort of rose might grow there well enough. And I saw no men there, and no children.'

★ ★ ★ ★ ★ ★ ★ ★ ★ ★ ★ ★

She drank again a shorter draught and turned over lightly but painfully. But she could not sleep or die just yet. For an hour or so Herbert sat by her, watching; her limbs shuddered now and then with a slow general spasm, as though cold or outtired; but there were no symptoms of a sharper torment. A faint savour of flowers mixed with the smell of drugs as the whitening dusk with the yellow twilight of the lamps. The place seemed ready swept and garnished for death to enter: the light had red and yellow colours as of blood and fog. The watcher felt sad and sick and half afraid; his mind was full of dim and bitter things. He was not in heart to pray; if indeed prayer could have undone things past, he might have believed it could break and remould the inevitable future growing minute by minute into the irrevocable present. The moments as they went seemed to touch him like falling drops of sand or water: as though the hourglass or the waterclock were indeed emptied by grains or gouts upon his head: a clock measuring its minutes by blood or tears instead of water or sand. He seemed in the dim hours to hear her pulses and his own. That night, as hope and trust fell away from under him, he first learnt the reality of fate: inevitable, not to be cajoled by resignation, not to be averted by intercession: unlike a God, incapable of wrath as of pity, not given to preference of evil or good, not liable to repentance or to change.

It was after dawn when Lesbia spoke next. 'Keep the curtains drawn,' she said; 'I won't see the sun again. I mean to die by lamplight.' Then after a little: 'The room must be dark and warm still, as I like it; though I am getting cold; at last. It will be close and dark enough soon; when I have got to bed again. Keep the light out. There: goodbye.' With this she put her hand out, dropped it, turned her face into the cushion, sighing, opened her eyes, and died. He left her in half an hour to the women, having kissed her only twice.

And that was the last of Lesbia Brandon, poetess and pagan.

## 26

## Passages from
## DENYS L'AUXERROIS
### *Walter Pater*

. . . Young lords prided themselves on saying that labour should have its ease, and were almost prepared to take freedom, plebeian freedom, (of course duly decorated, at least with wild-flowers) for a bride. For in truth Denys at his stall was turning the grave, slow movement of politic heads into a wild social license, which for a while made life like a stage-play. He first led those long processions, through which by and by 'the little people,' the discontented, the despairing, would utter their minds. One man engaged with another in talk in the market-place; a new influence came forth at the contact; another and then another adhered; at last a new spirit was abroad everywhere. The hot nights were noisy with swarming troops of dishevelled women and youths with red-stained lips and faces, carrying their lighted torches over the vine-clad hills, or rushing down the streets, to the horror of timid watchers, towards the cool spaces by the river. A shrill music, a laughter at all things, was everywhere. And the new spirit repaired even to church to take part in the novel offices of the Feast of Fools. Heads flung back in ecstasy – the morning sleep among the vines, when the fatigue of the night was over – dew-drenched garments – the serf lying at his ease at last: the artists, then so numerous at the place, caught what they could, something, at least, of the richness, the flexibility of the visible aspects of life, from all this. With them the life of seeming idleness, to which Denys was conducting the youth of Auxerre so pleasantly, counted but as the cultivation, for their due service to man, of delightful natural things. And the powers of nature concurred. It seemed there would be winter no more. The planet Mars drew nearer to the earth than usual, hanging in the low sky like a fiery red lamp. A massive but well-nigh lifeless vine on the wall of the cloister, allowed to remain there only as a curiosity on account of its immense age, in that *great* season, as it was long after called, clothed itself with fruit once more. The culture of the grape greatly increased. The sunlight fell for the first time on many a spot of deep woodland cleared for vine-growing; though Denys, a lover of trees, was careful to leave a stately specimen of forest growth here and there.

When his troubles came, one characteristic that had seemed most amiable in his prosperity was turned against him – a fondness for oddly grown or even misshapen, yet potentially happy, children; for odd animals also: he sympathised with them all, was skilful in healing their maladies, saved the hare in the chase, and sold his mantle to redeem a lamb from the butcher. He taught the people not to be afraid of the strange, ugly creatures which the light of the moving torches drew from their hiding-places, nor think it a bad omen that they approached. He tamed a veritable wolf to keep him company like a dog. It was the first of many ambiguous circumstances about him, from which, in the minds of an increasing number of people, a deep suspicion and hatred began to define itself. The rich *bestiary*, then compiling in the library of the great church, became, through his assistance, nothing less than a garden of Eden – the garden of Eden grown wild. The owl alone he abhorred. A little later, almost as if in revenge, alone of all animals it clung to him, haunting him persistently among the dusky stone towers, when grown gentler than ever he dared not kill it. He moved unhurt in the famous *ménagerie* of the castle, of which the common people were so much afraid, and let out the lions, themselves timid prisoners enough, through the streets during the fair. The incident suggested to the somewhat barren penmen of the day a 'morality' adapted from the old pagan books – a stage-play in which the God of Wine should return in triumph from the East. In the cathedral square the pageant was presented, amid an intolerable noise of every kind of pipe-music, with Denys in the chief part, upon a gaily-painted chariot, in soft silken raiment, and, for headdress, a strange elephant-scalp with gilded tusks.

And that unrivalled fairness and freshness of aspect: – how

did he alone preserve it untouched, through the wind and heat? In truth, it was not by magic, as some said, but by a natural simplicity in his living. When that dark season of his troubles arrived he was heard begging querulously one wintry night, 'Give me wine, meat; dark wine and brown meat!' – come back to the rude door of his old home in the cliff-side. Till that time the great vine-dresser himself drank only water; he had lived on spring-water and fruit. A lover of fertility in all its forms, in what did but suggest it, he was curious and penetrative concerning the habits of water, and had the secret of the divining-rod. Long before it came he could detect the scent of rain from afar, and would climb with delight to the great scaffolding on the unfinished tower to watch its coming over the thirsty vine-land, till it rattled on the great tiled roof of the church below; and then, throwing off his mantle, allow it to bathe his limbs freely, clinging firmly against the tempestuous wind among the carved imageries of dark stone.

It was on his sudden return after a long journey, (one of many inexplicable disappearances) coming back changed somewhat, that he ate flesh for the first time, tearing the hot, red morsels with his delicate fingers in a kind of wild greed. He had fled to the south from the first forbidding days of a hard winter which came at last. At the great seaport of Marseilles he had trafficked with sailors from all parts of the world, from Arabia and India, and bought their wares, exposed now for sale, to the wonder of all, at the Easter fair – richer wines and incense than had been known in Auxerre, seeds of marvellous new flowers, creatures wild and tame, new pottery painted in raw gaudy tints, the skins of animals, meats fried with unheard-of condiments. His stall formed a strange, unwonted patch of colour, found suddenly displayed in the hot morning.

★ ★ ★ ★ ★ ★ ★ ★ ★ ★ ★ ★

A kind of degeneration, of coarseness – the coarseness of satiety, and shapeless, battered-out appetite – with an almost savage taste for carnivorous diet, had come over the company. A rumour went abroad of certain women who had drowned, in mere wantonness, their new-born babes. A girl with child was found hanged by her own act in a dark cellar. Ah! if Denys also had not felt himself mad! But when the guilt of a murder, committed with a great vine-axe far out among the vineyards, was attributed vaguely to him, he could but wonder whether it had indeed been thus, and the shadow of a fancied crime abode with him. People turned against their favourite, whose former charms must now be counted only as the fascinations of witchcraft. It was as if the wine poured out for them had soured in the cup. The golden age had indeed come back for a while: – golden was it, or gilded only, after all? and they were too sick, or at least too serious, to carry through their parts in it. The monk Hermes was whimsically reminded of that *after-thought* in pagan poetry, of a Wine-god who had been in hell. Denys certainly, with all his flaxen fairness about him, was manifestly a sufferer. At first he thought of departing secretly to some other place. Alas! his wits were too far gone for certainty of success in the attempt. He feared to be brought back a prisoner. Those fat years were over. It was a time of scarcity. The working people might not eat and drink of the good things they had helped to store away. Tears rose in the eyes of needy children, of old or weak people like children, as they woke up again and again to sunless, frost-bound ruinous mornings; and the little hungry creatures wet prowling after scattered hedge-nuts or dried vine-tendrils. Mysterious, dark rains prevailed throughout the summer. The great offices of Saint John were fumbled through in a sudden darkness of unseasonable storm, which greatly damaged the carved ornaments of the church, the bishop reading his midday Mass by the light of the candle at his book. And then, one night, the night which seemed literally to have swallowed up the shortest day of the year, a plot was contrived by certain persons to take Denys as he went and kill him privately for a sorcerer. He could hardly tell how he escaped, and found himself safe in his earliest home, the cottage in the cliff-side, with such a big fire as he delighted in burning upon the hearth. They made a little feast as well as they could for the beautiful hunted creature, with abundance of waxlights.

★ ★ ★ ★ ★ ★ ★ ★ ★ ★ ★ ★

The religious ceremony was followed by a civic festival, in which Auxerre welcomed its future lord. The festival was to end at nightfall with a somewhat rude popular pageant, in which the person of Winter would be hunted blindfold through the streets. It was the sequel to that earlier stage-play of the *Return from the East* in which Denys had been the central figure. The old forgotten player saw his part before him, and, as if mechanically, fell again into the chief place, monk's dress and all. It might restore his popularity: who could tell? Hastily he donned the ashen-grey mantle, the rough haircloth about the throat, and went through the preliminary matter. And it happened that a point of the haircloth scratched his lip deeply, with a long trickling of blood upon the chin. It was as if the sight of blood transported the spectators with a kind of mad rage, and suddenly revealed to them the truth. The pretended hunting of the unholy creature became a real one, which brought out, in rapid increase, men's evil passions. The soul of Denys was already at rest, as his body, now borne along in front of the crowd, was tossed hither and thither, torn at last limb from limb. The men stuck little shreds of his flesh, or, failing that, of his torn raiment, into their caps; the women lending their long hairpins for the purpose. The monk Hermes sought in vain next day for any remains of the body of his friend. Only, at nightfall, the heart of Denys was brought to him by a stranger, still entire. It must long since have mouldered into dust under the stone, marked with a cross, where he buried it in a dark corner of the cathedral aisle.

## 27

## Extract from THE PICTURE OF DORIAN GRAY

*Oscar Wilde*

from Chapter XVI

It is said that passion makes one think in a circle. Certainly with hideous iteration the bitten lips of Dorian Gray shaped and reshaped those subtle words that dealt with soul and sense, till he had found in them the full expression, as it were, of his mood, and justified, by intellectual approval, passions that without such justification would still have dominated his temper. From cell to cell of his brain crept the one thought; and the wild desire to live, most terrible of all men's appetites, quickened into force each trembling nerve and fibre. Ugliness that had once been hateful to him because it made things real, became dear to him for that very same reason. Ugliness was the one reality. The coarse brawl, the loathsome den, the crude violence of disordered life, the very vileness of thief and outcast, were more vivid, in their intense actuality of impression, than all the gracious shapes of Art, the dreamy shadows of Song. They were what he needed for forgetfulness. In three days he would be free.

Suddenly the man drew up with a jerk at the top of a dark lane. Over the low roofs and jagged chimney stacks of the houses rose the black masts of ships. Wreaths of white mist clung like ghostly sails to the yards.

'Somewhere about here, sir, ain't it?' he asked huskily through the trap.

Dorian started, and peered around. 'This will do,' he answered, and, having got out hastily, and given the driver the extra fare he had promised him, he walked quickly in the direction of the quay. Here and there a lantern gleamed at the stern of some huge merchantman. The light shook and splintered in the puddles. A red glare came from an outward-bound steamer that was coaling. The slimy pavement looked like a wet mackintosh.

He hurried onwards toward the left, glancing back now and then to see if he was being followed. In about seven or eight minutes he reached a small shabby house, that was wedged in between two gaunt factories. In one of the top windows stood a lamp. He stopped, and gave a peculiar knock.

After a little time he heard steps in the passage, and the chain being unhooked. The door opened quietly, and he went in without saying a word to the squat misshapen figure that flattened itself into the shadow as he passed. At the end of the hall hung a tattered green curtain that swayed and shook in the gusty wind which had followed him in from the street. He dragged it aside, and entered a long, low room which looked as if it had once been a third-rate dancing saloon. Shrill flaring gas-jets, dulled and distorted in the fly-blown mirrors that faced them, were ranged about the walls. Greasy reflectors of ribbed tin backed them, making quivering discs of light. The floor was covered with ochre-coloured sawdust, trampled here and there into mud, and stained with dark rings of spilt liquor. Some Malays were crouching by a little charcoal stove playing with bone counters and showing their white teeth as they chattered. In one corner, with his head buried in his arms, a sailor sprawled over a table, and by the tawdrily-painted bar that ran across one complete side stood two haggard women mocking an old man who was brushing the sleeves of his coat with an expression of disgust. 'He thinks he's got red ants on him,' laughed one of them, as Dorian passed by. The man looked at her in terror and began to whimper.

At the end of the room there was a little staircase, leading to a darkened chamber. As Dorian hurried up its three rickety steps, the heavy odour of opium met him. He heaved a deep breath, and his nostrils quivered with pleasure. When he entered, a young man with smooth yellow hair, who was bending over a lamp, lighting a long thin pipe, looked up at him, and nodded in a hesitating manner.

'You here, Adrian?' muttered Dorian.

'Where else should I be?' he answered, listlessly. 'None of the chaps will speak to me now.'

'I thought you had left England.'

'Darlington is not going to do anything. My brother paid the bill at last. George doesn't speak to me either . . . I don't care,' he added, with a sigh. 'As long as one has this stuff, one doesn't want friends. I think I have had too many friends.'

Dorian winced, and looked round at the grotesque things that lay in such fantastic postures on the ragged mattresses. The twisted limbs, the gaping mouths, the staring lustreless eyes, fascinated him. He knew in what strange heavens they were suffering, and what dull hells were teaching them the secret of some new joy. They were better off than he was. He was prisoned in thought. Memory, like a horrible malady, was eating his soul away. From time to time he seemed to see the eyes of Basil Hallward looking at him. Yet he felt he could not stay. The presence of Adrian Singleton troubled him. He wanted to be where no man would know who he was. He wanted to escape from himself.

'I am going on to the other place,' he said, after a pause.

'On the wharf?'

'Yes.'

'That mad-cat is sure to be there. They won't have her in this place now.'

Dorian shrugged his shoulders. 'I am sick of women who love one. Women who hate one are much more interesting. Besides, the stuff is better.'

'Much the same.'

'I like it better. Come and have something to drink. I must have something.'

'I don't want anything,' murmured the young man.

'Never mind.'

Adrian Singleton rose up wearily, and followed Dorian to the bar. A half-caste, in a ragged turban and a shabby ulster, grinned a hideous greeting as he thrust a bottle of brandy and two tumblers in front of them. The women sidled up, and began to chatter. Dorian turned his back on them, and said something in a low voice to Adrian Singleton.

A crooked smile, like a Malay crease, writhed across the face of one of the women.

'We are very proud to-night,' she sneered.

'For God's sake don't talk to me,' cried Dorian, stamping his foot on the ground. 'What do you want? Money? Here it is. Don't ever talk to me again.'

Two red sparks flashed for a moment in the woman's sodden eyes, then flickered out, and left them dull and glazed. She tossed her head, and raked the coins off the counter with greedy fingers. Her companion watched her enviously.

'It's no use,' sighed Adrian Singleton. 'I don't care to go back. What does it matter? I am quite happy here.'

'You will write to me if you want anything, won't you?' said Dorian, after a pause.

'Perhaps.'

'Good-night, then.'

'Good-night,' answered the young man, passing up the steps, and wiping his parched mouth with a handkerchief.

Dorian walked to the door with a look of pain in his face. As he drew the curtain aside a hideous laugh broke from the painted lips of the woman who had taken his money. 'There goes the devil's bargain!' she hiccoughed, in a hoarse voice.

'Curse you!' he answered, 'don't call me that.'

She snapped her fingers. 'Prince Charming is what you like to be called, ain't it?' she yelled after him.

The drowsy sailor leapt to his feet as she spoke, and looked wildly round. The sound of the shutting of the hall door fell on his ear. He rushed out as if in pursuit.

Dorian Gray hurried along the quay through the drizzling rain. His meeting with Adrian Singleton had strangely moved him, and he wondered if the ruin of that young life was really to be laid at his door, as Basil Hallward had said to him with such infamy of insult. He bit his lip, and for a few seconds his eyes grew sad. Yet, after all, what did it matter to him? One's days were too brief to take the burden of another's errors on one's shoulders. Each man lived his own life, and paid his own price for living it. The only pity was one had to pay so often for a single fault. One had to pay over and over again, indeed. In her dealings with man Destiny never closed her accounts.

There are moments, psychologists tell us, when the passion for sin, or for what the world calls sin, so dominates a nature, that every fibre of the body, as every cell of the brain, seems to be instinct with fearful impulses. Men and women at such moments lose the freedom of their will. They move to their terrible end as automatons move. Choice is taken from them, and conscience is either killed, or, if it lives at all, lives but to give rebellion its fascination, and disobedience its charm. For all sins, as theologians weary not of reminding us, are sins of disobedience. When that high spirit, that morning-star of evil, fell from heaven, it was as a rebel that he fell.

Callous, concentrated on evil, with stained mien, and soul hungry for rebellion, Dorian Gray hastened on, quickening his step as he went, but as he darted aside into a dim archway, that had served him often as a short cut to the ill-famed place where he was going, he felt himself suddenly seized from behind, and before he had time to defend himself he was thrust back against the wall, with a brutal hand round his throat.

## 28

## A LAST WORD

*Ernest Dowson*

Let us go hence: the night is now at hand;
   The day is overworn, the birds all flown;
   And we have reaped the crops the gods have sown;
Despair and death; deep darkness o'er the land,

Broods like an owl; we cannot understand
   Laughter or tears, for we have only known
   Surpassing vanity: vain things alone
Have driven our perverse and aimless band.

Let us go hence, somewhither strange and cold,
   To Hollow Lands where just men and unjust
   Find end of labour, where's rest for the old,
Freedom to all from love and fear and lust.
Twine our torn hands! O pray the earth enfold
Our life-sick hearts and turn them into dust.

## 29

## THE ABSINTHE-DRINKER

***Arthur Symons***

Gently I wave the visible world away
Far off, I hear a roar, afar yet near,
Far off and strange, a voice in my ear,
And is the voice my own? the words I say
Fall strangely, like a dream, a cross the day;
And the dim sunshine is a dream. How clear,
New as the world to lovers' eyes, appear
The men and women passing on their way!

The world is very fair. The hours are all
Linked in a dance of mere forgetfulness.
I am at peace with God and man. O glide,
Sands of the hour-glass that I count not, fall
Serenely: scarce I feel your soft caress,
Rocked on this dreamy and indifferent tide.

## 30

# Passages from THE CULTURED FAUN

*Lionel Johnson*

. . . That is the point: exquisite appreciation of pain, exquisite thrills of anguish, exquisite adoration of suffering. Here comes in a tender patronage of Catholicism: white tapers upon the high altar, an ascetic and beautiful young priest, the great gilt monstrance, the subtle-scented and mystical incense, the old world accents of the Vulgate, of the Holy Offices; the splendour of the sacred vestments. We kneel at some hour, not too early for our convenience, repeating the solemn Latin, drinking in those Gregorian tones, with plenty of modern French sonnets in memory, should the sermon be dull. But to join the Church! Ah, no! better to dally with the enchanting mysteries, to pass from our dreams of delirium to our dreams of sanctity with no coarse facts to jar upon us. And so these refined persons cherish a double 'passion', the sentiment of repentant yearning and the sentiment of rebellious sin.

To play the part properly a flavour of cynicism is recommended: a scientific profession of materialist dogmas, coupled – for you should forswear consistency – with gloomy chatter about 'The Will to Live' . . . Jumble all these 'impressions' together, your sympathies and your sorrows, your devotion and your despair; carry them about with you in a state of fermentation, and finally conclude that life is loathsome yet that beauty is beatific. And beauty – ah, beauty is everything beautiful! Isn't that a trifle obvious, you say? That is the charm of it, it shows your perfect simplicity, your chaste and catholic innocence. Innocence of course: beauty is always innocent, ultimately. No doubt there are 'monstrous' things, terrible pains, the haggard eyes of an *absintheur*, the pallid faces of 'neurotic' sinners; but all that is the portion of our Parisian friends, such and such a 'group of artists', who meet at the Café So-and-So. We like people to think we are much the same, but it isn't true. We are quite harmless, we only concoct strange and subtle verse about it. And, anyway, beauty includes everything; there's another sweet saying for you from our 'impressionist' copy-books. Impressions! that is all. Life is mean and vulgar, Members of Parliament are odious, the critics are commercial pedants: we alone know Beauty, and Art, and Sorrow and Sin. Impressions! exquisite, dainty fantasies; fiery-coloured visions; and impertinence struggling into epigram, for 'the true' criticism; *c'est adorable!*

★ ★ ★ ★ ★ ★ ★ ★ ★ ★ ★ ★

We are the Elect of Beauty: saints and sinners, devils and devotees, Athenians and Parisians, Romans of the Empire and Italians of the Renaissance. *Fin de siècle! Fin de siècle!* Literature is a thing of beauty, blood, and nerves.

## 31

## THE DECADENT TO HIS SOUL

*Richard Le Gallienne*

The Decadent was speaking to his soul –
Poor useless thing, he said,
Why did God burden me with such as thou?
The body were enough
The body gives me all.

The soul's a sort of sentimental wife
That prays and whimpers of the higher life,
Objects to latch-keys, and bewails the old,
The dear old days, of passion and of dream,
When life was a blank canvas, yet untouched
Of the great painter Sin.

Yet, little soul, thou hast fine eyes,
And knowest fine airy motions,
Hast a voice –
Why wilt thou so devote them to the church?

His face grew strangely sweet –
As when a toad smiles.
He dreamed of a new sin:
An incest 'twixt the body and the soul.

He drugged his soul, and in a house of sin
She played all she remembered out of heaven
For him to kiss and clip by.
He took a little harlot in his hands,
And she made all his veins like boiling oil,
Then that grave organ made them cool again.

Then from that day, he used his soul
As bitters to the over dulcet sins,

As olives to the fatness of the feast –
She made those dear heart-breaking ecstasies
Of minor chords amid the Phrygian lutes,
She sauced his sins with splendid memories,
Starry regrets and infinite hopes and fears;
His holy youth and his first love
Made pearly background to strange-coloured vice.

Sin is no sin when virtue is forgot.
It is so good in sin to keep in sight
The white hills whence we fell, to measure by –
To say I was so high, so white, so pure,
And am so low, so blood-stained and so base;
I revel here amid the sweet sweet mire
And yonder are the hills of morning flowers:
So high, so low; so lost and with me yet;
To stretch the octave 'twixt the dream and deed,
Ah, that's the thrill!

To dream so well, to do so ill, –
There comes the bitter-sweet that makes the sin.

First drink the stars, then grunt amid the mire,
So shall the mire have something of the stars,
And the high stars be fragrant of the mire.

The Decadent was speaking to his soul –
Dear witch, I said the body was enough.
How young, how simple as a suckling child!
And then I dreamed – 'an incest 'twixt the body and the
soul:'
Let's wed, I thought, the seraph with the dog,
And wait the purple thing that shall be born.

And now look round – seest thou this bloom?
Seven petals and each petal seven dyes,
The stem is gilded and the root in blood:
That came of thee.

Yea, all my flowers were single save for thee.
I pluck seven fruits from off a single tree,
I pluck seven flowers from off a single stem,
I light my palace with the seven stars,
And eat strange dishes to Gregorian chants:
All thanks to thee.

But the soul wept with hollow hectic face,
Captive in that lupanar of a man.
And I who passed by heard and wept for both, –
The man was once an apple-cheek dear lad,
The soul was once an angel up in heaven.

O let the body be a healthy beast,
And keep the soul a singing soaring bird;
But lure thou not the soul from out the sky
To pipe unto the body in the sty.

## 32

## Passages from A DEFENCE OF COSMETICS

***Sir Max Beerbohm***

For behold! The Victorian era comes to its end and the day of sancta simplicitas is quite ended. The old signs are here and the portents to warn the seer of life that we are ripe for a new epoch of artifice. Are not men rattling the dice-box and ladies dipping their fingers in the rouge-pot? At Rome, in the keenest time of her degringolade, when there was gambling even in the holy temples, great ladies (does not Lucian tell us?) did not scruple to squander all they had upon unguents from Arabia. Nero's mistresses and unhappy wife, Poppaea, of shameful memory, had in her travelling retinue fifteen – or, as some say, fifty – she-asses, for the sake of their milk, that was thought an incomparable guard against cosmetics with poison in them. Last century, too, when life was lived by candle-light, and ethics was but etiquette, and even art a question of punctilio, women, we know, gave the best hours of the day to the crafty farding of their faces and the towering of their coiffures. And men, throwing passion into the wine-bowl to sink or swim, turned out thought to browse upon the green cloth.

★ ★ ★ ★ ★ ★ ★ ★ ★ ★ ★ ★

And this – say you? – will make monotony? You are mistaken, *toto coelo* mistaken. When your mistress has wearied you with one expression, then it will need but a few touches of that pencil, a backward sweep of that brush, and lo, you will be revelling in another. For though, of course, the painting of the face is, in manner, most like the painting of canvas, in outcome, it is rather akin to the art of music – lasting, like music's echo, not for very long. So that, no doubt, of the many little appurtenances of the Reformed Toilet Table, not the least vital will be a list of the emotions that become its owner, with recipes for simulating them. According to the colour she wills her hair to be for the time – black or yellow or, peradventure, burnished red – she will blush for you, sneer for you, laugh or languish for you. The good combinations of line and colour are nearly numberless, and by their means poor restless woman will be able to realise her moods in all their shades and lights and dappledoms, to live many lives and masquerade through many moments of joy. No monotony will be. And for us men matrimony will have lost its sting.

But that in the world of women they will not neglect this art, so ripping in itself, in its result so wonderfully beneficent, I am sure indeed. Much, I have said, is already done for its full revival. The spirit of the age has made straight the path of its professors. Fashion has made Jezebel surrender her monopoly of the rouge-pot. As yet, the great art of self-embellishment is but in its infancy. But if Englishwomen can bring it to the flower of an excellence so supreme as never yet has it known, then, though Old England lose her martial and commercial supremacy, we patriots will have the satisfaction of knowing that she has been advanced at one bound to a place in the councils of aesthetic Europe. And, in sooth, is this hoping too high of my countrywomen? True that, as the art seems always to have appealed to the ladies of Athens, and it was not until the waning time of the Republic that Roman ladies learned to love the practice of it, so Paris, Athenian in this as in all other things, has been noted hitherto as a far more vivid centre of the art than London. But it was in Rome, under the Emperors, that unguentaria reached its zenith, and shall it not be in London, soon, that unguentaria shall outstrip its Roman perfection!

★ ★ ★ ★ ★ ★ ★ ★ ★ ★ ★ ★

Loveliness shall sit at the toilet, watching her oval face in the oval mirror. Her smooth fingers shall flit among the paints and powder, to tip and mingle them, catch up a pencil, clasp a phial, and what not and what not, until the mask of vermeil tinct has been laid aptly, the enamel quite hardened. And, heavens, how she will [ ] us and ensorcel our eyes! Positively rouge will rob us for a time of all our reason; we shall go mad over masks. Was it not at Capua that they had a whole street where nothing was sold but dyes and unguents? We must have such a street, and, to fill our new Splasia; our Arcade of the Unguents, all herbs and minerals and live creatures shall give of their substance. The white cliffs of Albion shall be ground to powder for Loveliness, and perfumed by the ghosts of many a little violet. The fluffy eider-ducks, that are swimming round the pond, shall lose their feathers, that the powder-puff may be moonlike as it passes over Loveliness's lovely face. Even the camels shall become ministers of delight, giving many tufts of their hair to be stained in her splendid colour-box, and across her cheek the swift hare's foot shall fly as of old. The sea shall offer her the phucus, its scarlet weed. We shall spill the blood of mulberries at her bidding. And, as in another period of great ecstasy, a dancing wanton, le belle Aubrey, was crowned upon a church's lighted altar, so Arsenic, that 'greentress'd goddess,' ashamed at length of skulking between the soup of the unpopular and the test-tubes of the Queen's analyst, shall be exalted to a place of consummate honour upon the toilet-table of Loveliness.

## 33

## DREGS

*Ernest Dowson*

The fire is out, and spent the warmth thereof,
(This is the end of every song man sings!)
The golden wine is drunk, the dregs remain,
Bitter as wormwood and as salt as pain;
And health and hope have gone the way of love
Into the drear oblivion of lost things.
Ghosts go along with us until the end;
This was a mistress, this, perhaps, a friend.
With pale, indifferent eyes, we sit and wait
For the dropt curtain and the closing gate:
This is the end of all the songs man sings.

## 34

## NIHILISM

*Lionel Johnson*

Among immortal things not made with hands;
Among immortal things, dead hands have made:
Under the Heavens, upon the Earth, there stands
Man's life, my life: of life I am afraid.

Where silent things, and unimpassioned things,
Where things of nought, and things decaying, are:
I shall be calm soon, with the calm, death brings.
The skies are gray there, without any star.

Only the rest! the rest! Only the gloom,
Soft and long gloom! The pausing from all thought!
My life, I cannot taste: the eternal tomb
Brings me the peace, which life has never brought.

For all the things I do, and do not well;
All the forced drawings of a mortal breath:
Are as the hollow music of a bell,
That times the slow approach of perfect death.

## 35

## THE OPIUM-SMOKER

*Arthur Symons*

I am engulfed, and drown deliciously.
Soft music like a perfume, and sweet light
Golden with audible colours exquisite,
Swathe me with cerements for eternity.
Time is no more. I pause and yet I flee.
A million ages wrap me round with night.
I drain a million ages of delight.
I hold the future in my memory.

Also, I have this garret which I rent,
This bed of straw, and this that was a chair,
This worn-out body like a tattered tent,
This crust, of which the rats have eaten part,
This pipe of opium; rage, remorse, despair;
This soul at pawn and this delirious heart.

## 36

## Passages from THE GREAT GOD PAN

*Arthur Machen*

. . . 'I hope the smell doesn't annoy you, Clarke; there's nothing unwholesome about it. It may make you a bit sleepy, that's all.'

Clarke heard the words quite distinctly, and knew that Raymond was speaking to him, but for the life of him he could not rouse himself from his lethargy. He could only think of the lonely walk he had taken fifteen years ago; it was his last look at the fields and woods he had known since he was a child, and now it all stood out in brilliant light, as a picture, before him. Above all there came to his nostrils the scent of summer, the smell of flowers mingled, and the odour of the woods, of cool shaded places, deep in the green depths, drawn forth by the sun's heat; and the scent of the good earth, lying as it were with arms stretched forth, and smiling lips, overpowered all. His fancies made him wander, as he had wandered long ago, from the fields into the wood, tracking a little path between the shining undergrowth of beech-trees; and the trickle of water dropping from the limestone rock sounded as a clear melody in the dream. Thoughts began to go astray and to mingle with other recollections; the beech alley was transformed to a path beneath ilex-trees, and here and there a vine climbed from bough to bough, and sent up waving tendrils and drooped with purple grapes, and the sparse grey-green leaves of a wild olive-tree stood out against the dark shadows of the ilex. Clarke, in the deep folds of dream, was conscious that the path from his father's house had led him into an undiscovered country, and he was wondering at the strangeness of it all, when suddenly, in place of the hum and murmur of the summer, an infinite silence seemed to fall on all things, and the wood was hushed, and for a moment of time he stood face to face there with a presence, that was neither man nor beast, neither the living nor the dead, but all things mingled, the form of all things but devoid of all form. And in that moment, the sacrament of body and soul was dissolved, and a voice seemed to cry 'Let us go hence,' and then the darkness beyond the stars, the darkness of everlasting.

When Clarke woke up with a start he saw Raymond pouring a few drops of some oily fluid into a green phial, which he stoppered tightly.

'You have been dozing,' he said: 'the journey must have tired you out. It is done now. I am going to fetch Mary; I shall be back in ten minutes.'

Clarke lay back in his chair and wondered. It seemed as if he had but passed from one dream into another. He half expected to see the walls of the laboratory melt and disappear, and to awake in London, shuddering at his own sleeping fancies. But at last the door opened, and the doctor returned, and behind him came a girl of about seventeen, dressed all in white. She was so beautiful that Clarke did not wonder at what the doctor had written to him. She was blushing now over face and neck and arms, but Raymond seemed unmoved.

'Mary,' he said, 'the time has come. You are quite free. Are you willing to trust yourself to me entirely?'

'Yes, dear.'

'You hear that, Clarke? You are my witness. Here is the chair, Mary. It is quite easy. Just sit in and lean back. Are you ready?'

'Yes, dear, quite ready. Give me a kiss before you begin.'

The doctor stooped and kissed her mouth, kindly enough. 'Now shut your eyes,' he said. The girl closed her eyelids, as if she were tired, and longed for sleep, and Raymond held the green phial to her nostrils. Her face grew white, whiter than her dress; she struggled faintly, and then with the feeling of submission strong within her, crossed her arms upon her breast as a little child about to say her prayers. The bright light of the lamp beam fell upon her, and Clarke watched changes fleeting over that face as the changes of the hills when the summer clouds float across the sun. And then she lay all white and still, and the doctor turned up one of her eyelids. She was quite unconscious. Raymond pressed hard on one of the levers and the chair instantly sank back. Clarke saw him cutting away a circle, like a tonsure, from her hair, and the lamp was moved nearer. Raymond took a small glittering instrument from a little case, and Clarke turned away shuddering. When he looked again the doctor was binding up the wound he had made.

'She will awake in five minutes.' Raymond was still perfectly cool. 'There is nothing more to be done; we can only wait.'

The minutes passed slowly; they could hear a slow, heavy ticking. There was an old clock in the passage. Clarke felt sick and faint; his knees shook beneath him, he could hardly stand.

Suddenly, as they watched, they heard a long-drawn sigh, and suddenly did the colour that had vanished return to the girl's cheeks, and suddenly her eyes opened. Clarke quailed before them. They shone with an awful light, looking far away, and a great wonder fell upon her face, and her hands stretched out as if to touch what was invisible; but in an instant the wonder faded, and gave place to the most awful terror. The muscles of her face were hideously convulsed, she shook from head to foot; the soul seemed struggling and shuddering within the house of flesh. It was a horrible sight, and Clarke rushed forward, as she fell shrieking to the floor.

Three days later Raymond took Clarke to Mary's bedside. She was lying wide-awake, rolling her head from side to side, and grinning vacantly.

'Yes,' said the doctor, still quite cool, 'it is a great pity; she is a hopeless idiot. However, it could not be helped; and, after all, she has seen the Great God Pan.'

★ ★ ★ ★ ★ ★ ★ ★ ★ ★ ★ ★

*Singular narrative told me by my Friend, Dr. Phillips. He assures me that all the facts related therein are strictly and wholly True, but refuses to give either the Surnames of the Persons concerned, or the Place where these Extraordinary Events occurred.*

Mr. Clarke began to read over the account for the tenth time, glancing now and then at the pencil notes he had made when it was told him by his friend. It was one of his humours to pride himself on a certain literary ability; he thought well of his style, and took pains in arranging the circumstances in dramatic order. He read the following story: –

The persons concerned in this statement are Helen V., who, if she is still alive, must now be a woman of twenty-three, Rachel M., since deceased, who was a year younger than the above, and Trevor W., an imbecile, aged eighteen. These persons were at the period of the story inhabitants of a village on the borders of Wales, a place of some importance in the time of the Roman occupation, but now a scattered hamlet, of not more than five hundred souls. It is situated on rising ground, about six miles from the sea, and is sheltered by a large and picturesque forest.

Some eleven years ago, Helen V. came to the village under rather peculiar circumstances. It is understood that she, being an orphan, was adopted in her infancy by a distant relative, who brought her up in his own house till she was twelve years old. Thinking, however, that it would be better for the child to have playmates of her own age, he advertised in several local papers for a good home in a comfortable farmhouse for a girl of twelve, and this advertisement was answered by Mr. R., a well-to-do farmer in the above-mentioned village. His references proving satisfactory, the gentleman sent his adopted daughter to Mr. R., with a letter, in which he stipulated that her guardians need be at no trouble in the matter of education, as she was already sufficiently educated for the position in life which she would occupy. In fact, Mr. R. was given to understand that the girl was to be allowed her own occupations, and to spend her time almost as she liked. Mr. R. duly met her at the nearest station, a town some seven miles away from his house, and seems to have remarked nothing extraordinary about the child, except that she was reticent as to her former life and her adopted father. She was, however, of a very different type from the inhabitants of the village; her skin was a pale, clear olive, and her features were strongly marked, and of a somewhat foreign character. She appears to have settled down easily enough into farmhouse life, and became a favourite with the children, who sometimes went with her on her rambles in the forest, for this was her amusement. Mr. R. states that he has known her to go out by herself directly after their early breakfast, and not return till after dusk, and that, feeling uneasy at a young girl being out alone for so many hours, he communicated with her adopted father, who replied in a brief note that Helen must do as she chose. In the winter, when the forest paths are impassable, she spent most of her time in her bedroom, where she slept alone, according to the instructions of her relative. It was on one of these expeditions to the forest that the first of the singular incidents with which this girl is connected occurred, the date being about a year after her arrival at the village. The preceding winter had been remarkably severe, the snow drifting to a great depth, and the frost continuing for an unexampled period, and the summer following was as noteworthy for its extreme heat. On one of the very hottest days in this summer, Helen V. left the farmhouse for one of her long rambles in the forest, taking with her, as usual, some bread and meat for lunch. She was seen by some men in the fields making for the old Roman Road, a green causeway which traverses the highest part of the wood, and they were astonished to observe that the girl had taken off her hat, though the heat of the sun was already almost tropical. As it happened, a labourer, Joseph W. by name, was working in the forest near the Roman Road, and at twelve o'clock his little son, Trevor, brought the man his dinner of bread and cheese. After the meal, the boy, who was about seven years old at the time, left his father at work, and, as he said, went to look for flowers in the wood, and the man, who could hear him shouting with delight over his discoveries, felt no uneasiness. Suddenly, however, he was horrified at hearing the most dreadful screams, evidently the result of great terror, proceeding from the direction in which his son had gone, and he hastily threw down his tools and ran to see what had happened. Tracing his path by the sound, he met the little boy, who was running headlong, and was evidently terribly frightened, and on questioning him the man at last elicited that after picking a posy of flowers he felt tired, and lay down on the grass and fell asleep. He was suddenly awakened, as he stated, by a peculiar noise, a sort of singing he called it, and on peeping through the branches he saw Helen V. playing on the grass with a 'strange naked man,' whom he seemed unable to describe more fully. He said he felt dreadfully frightened, and ran away crying for his father. Joseph W. proceeded in the direction indicated by his son, and found Helen V. sitting on the grass in the middle of a glade or open space left by charcoal burners. He angrily charged her with frightening his little boy, but she entirely denied the accusation and laughed at the child's story of a 'strange man,' to which he himself did not attach much credence. Joseph W. came to the conclusion that the boy had woke up with a sudden fright, as children sometimes do, but Trevor persisted in his story, and continued in such evident distress that at last his father took him home, hoping that his mother would be able to soothe him. For many weeks, however, the boy gave his parents much anxiety; he became nervous and strange in his manner, refusing to leave the cottage by himself, and constantly alarming the household by waking in the night with cries of 'The man in the wood! Father! Father!'

In course of time, however, the impression seemed to have worn off, and about three months later he accompanied his father to the house of a gentleman in the neighbourhood, for whom Joseph W. occasionally did work. The man was shown into the study, and the little boy was left sitting in the hall, and a few minutes later, while the gentleman was giving W. his instructions, they were both horrified by a piercing shriek and the sound of a fall, and rushing out they found the child lying senseless on the floor, his face contorted with terror. The doctor was immediately summoned, and after some examination he pronounced the child to be suffering from a kind of fit, apparently produced by a sudden shock. The boy was taken to one of the bedrooms, and after some time recovered consciousness, but only to pass into a condition described by the medical man as one of violent hysteria. The doctor exhibited a strong sedative, and in the course of two hours pronounced him fit to walk home, but in passing through the hall the paroxysms of fright returned and with additional violence. The father perceived that the child was pointing at some object and heard the old cry, 'The man in the wood,' and looking in the direction indicated saw a stone head of grotesque appearance, which had been built into the wall above one of the doors. It seems that the owner of the house had recently made alterations on his premises, and in digging the foundation for some offices, the men had found a curious head, evidently of the Roman period, which had been placed in the hall in the manner described. The head is pronounced by the most experienced archaeologists of the district to be that of a faun or satyr.

From whatever cause arising, this second shock seemed too severe for the boy Trevor, and at the present date he suffers from a weakness of intellect, which gives but little promise of amending. The matter caused a good deal of sensation at the time, and the girl Helen was closely questioned by Mr. R., but to no purpose, she steadfastly denying that she had frightened or in any way molested Trevor.

The second event with which this girl's name is connected took place about six years ago, and is of a still more extraordinary nature.

At the beginning of the summer of 1882 Helen contracted a friendship of a peculiarly intimate character with Rachel M., the daughter of a prosperous farmer in the neighbourhood. This girl, who was a year younger than Helen, was considered by most people to be the prettier of the two, though Helen's features had to a great extent softened as she became older. The two girls, who were together on every available opportunity, presented a singular contrast, the one with her clear, olive skin and almost Italian appearance, and the other of the proverbial red and white of our rural districts. It must be stated that the payments made to Mr. R. for the maintenance of Helen were known in the village for their excessive liberality, and the impression was general that she would one day inherit a large sum from her relative. The parents of Rachel were therefore not averse from their daughter's friendship with the girl, and even encouraged the intimacy, though they now bitterly regret having done so. Helen still retained her extraordinary fondness for the forest, and on several occasions Rachel accompanied her, the two friends setting out early in the morning, and remaining in the wood till dusk. Once or twice after these excursions Mrs. M. thought her daughter's manner rather peculiar; she seemed languid and dreamy, and as it has been expressed, 'different from herself,' but these peculiarities seemed to have been thought too trifling for remark. One evening, however, after Rachel had come home, her mother heard a noise which sounded like suppressed weeping in the girl's room, and on going in found her lying, half undressed, upon the bed, evidently in the greatest distress. As soon as she saw her mother, she exclaimed, 'Ah, Mother, Mother, why did you let me go to the forest with Helen?' Mrs M. was astonished at so strange a question, and proceeded to make inquiries. Rachel told her a wild story. She said –

Clarke closed the book with a snap, and turned his chair towards the fire. When his friend sat one evening in that very chair, and told his story, Clarke had interrupted him at a point a little subsequent to this, had cut short his words in a paroxysm of horror. 'My God!' he had exclaimed, 'think, think what you are saying. It is too incredible, too monstrous; such things can never be in this quiet world, where men and women live and die, and struggle, and conquer, or maybe fail, and fall down under sorrow, and grieve and suffer strange fortunes for many a year; but not this, Phillips, not such things as this. There must be some explanation, some way out of the terror. Why, man, if such a case were possible, our earth would be nightmare.'

But Phillips had told his story to the end, concluding:

'Her flight remains a mystery to this day; she vanished in broad sunlight; they saw her walking in a meadow, and a few moments later she was not there.'

Clarke had tried to conceive the thing again, as he sat by the fire, and again his mind shuddered and shrank back, appalled before the sight of such awful, unspeakable elements enthroned as it were, and triumphant in human flesh. Before him stretched the long dim vista of the green causeway in the forest, as his friend had described it; he saw the swaying leaves and the quivering shadows on the grass, he saw the sunlight and the flowers, and far away, far in the long distance, the two figures moved toward him. One was Rachel, but the other?

Clarke had tried his best to disbelieve it all, but at the end of the account, as he had written it in his book, he had placed the inscription:

ET DIABOLUS INCARNATUS EST.
ET HOMO FACTUS EST.

## 37

## POEM

*John Gray*

Geranium, houseleek, laid in oblong beds
On the trim grass. The daisies' leprous stain
Is fresh. Each night the daisies burst again,
Though every day the gardener crops their heads.

A wistful child, in foul unwholesome shreds,
Recalls some legend of a daisy chain
That makes a pretty necklace. She would fain
Make one, and wear it, if she had some threads.

Sun, leprous flowers, foul child. The asphalt burns.
The garrulous sparrows perch on metal Burns.
Sing! Sing! they say, and flutter with their wings.
He does not sing, he only wonders why
He is sitting there. The sparrows sing. And I
Yield to the strait allure of simple things.

## 38

## ENNUI

*Lord Alfred Douglas*

Alas! and oh that Spring should come again
Upon the soft wings of desired days,
And bring with her no anodyne to pain,
And no discernment of untroubled ways.
There was a time when her yet distant feet,
Guessed by some prescience more than half divine,
Gave to my listening ear such happy warning,
  That fresh, serene, and sweet,
My thoughts soared up like larks into the morning,
From the dew-sprinkled meadows crystalline.

Soared up into heights celestial,
And saw the whole world like a ball of fire,
Fashioned to be a monster playing ball
For the enchantment of my young desire.
And yesterday they flew to this black cloud,
(Missing the way to those ethereal spheres.)
And saw the earth a vision of affright,
  And men a sordid crowd,
And felt the fears and drank the bitter tears,
And saw the empty houses of Delight.

The sun has sunk into a moonless sea,
And every road leads down from Heaven to Hell,
The pearls are numbered on youth's rosary,
I have outlived the days desirable.
What is there left? And how shall dead men sing
Unto the loosened strings of Love and Hate,
Or take strong hands to Beauty's ravishment?
  Who shall devise this thing,
To give high utterance to Miscontent,
Or make Indifference articulate?

## 39

## Passages from ENOCH SOAMES

***Sir Max Beerbohm***

There, on that October evening – there, in that exuberant vista of gilding and crimson velvet set amidst all those opposing mirrors and upholding caryatids, with fumes of tobacco ever rising to the painted and pagan ceiling, and with the hum of presumably cynical conversation broken into so sharply now and again by the clatter of dominoes shuffled on marble tables, I drew a deep breath and, 'This indeed,' said I to myself, 'is life' (Forgive me that theory. Remember the waging of even the South African War was not yet.)

It was the hour before dinner. We drank vermuth. Those who knew Rothenstein were pointing him out to those who knew him only by name. Men were constantly coming in through the swing-doors and wandering slowly up and down in search of vacant tables or of tables occupied by friends. One of these rovers interested me because I was sure he wanted to catch Rothenstein's eye. He had twice passed our table, with a hesitating look; but Rothenstein, in the thick of a disquisition on Puvis de Chavannes, had not seen him. He was a stooping, shambling person, rather tall, very pale, with longish and brownish hair. He had a thin, vague beard, or, rather, he had a chin on which a large number of hairs weakly curled and clustered to cover its retreat. He was an odd-looking person; but in the nineties odd apparitions were more frequent, I think, than they are now. The young writers of that era – and I was sure this man was a writer – strove earnestly to be distinct in aspect. This man had striven unsuccessfully. He wore a soft black hat of the clerical kind, but of Bohemian intention, and a gray waterproof cape which, perhaps because it was waterproof, failed to be romantic. I decided that 'dim' was the mot juste for him. I had already essayed to write, and was immensely keen on the mot juste, that Holy Grail of the period.

The dim man was now again approaching our table, and this time he made up his mind to pause in front of it.

'You don't remember me,' he said in a toneless voice.

Rothenstein brightly focused him.

'Yes, I do,' he replied after a moment, with pride rather than effusion – pride in a retentive memory. 'Edwin Soames.'

'Enoch Soames,' said Enoch.

'Enoch Soames,' repeated Rothenstein in a tone implying that it was enough to have hit on the surname. 'We met in Paris a few times when you were living there. We met at the Café Groche.'

'And I came to your studio once.'

'Oh, yes; I was sorry I was out.'

'But you were in. You showed me some of your paintings, you know. I hear you're in Chelsea now.'

'Yes.'

I almost wondered that Mr. Soames did not, after this monosyllable, pass along. He stood patiently there, rather like a dumb animal, rather like a donkey looking over a gate. A sad figure, his. It occurred to me that 'hungry' was perhaps the mot juste for him; but – hungry for what? He looked as if he had little appetite for anything. I was sorry for him; and Rothenstein, though he had not invited him to Chelsea, did ask him to sit down and have something to drink.

Seated, he was more self-assertive. He flung back the wings of his cape with a gesture which, had not those wings been waterproof, might have seemed to hurl defiance at things in general. And he ordered an absinthe. 'Je me tiens toujours fidèle,' he told Rothenstein, 'a la sorcière glauque.'

'It is bad for you,' said Rothenstein, dryly.

'Nothing is bad for one,' answered Soames. 'Dans ce monde il n'y a ni bien ni mal.'

'Nothing good and nothing bad? How do you mean?'

'I explained it all in the preface to "Negations".'

' "Negations"?'

'Yes, I gave you a copy of it.'

'Oh yes, of course. But, did you explain, for instance, that there was no such thing as bad or good grammar?'

'N-no,' said Soames. 'Of course in art there is the good and the evil. But in life – no.' He was rolling a cigarette. He had weak, white hands, not well washed, and with finger-tips much stained with nicotine. 'In life there are illusions of good and evil, but' – his voice trailed away to a murmur in which the words 'vieux jeu' and 'rococo' were faintly audible. I think he felt he was not doing himself justice, and feared that Rothenstein was going to point out his fallacies. Anyhow, he cleared his throat and said, 'Parlons d'autre chose.'

It occurs to you that he was a fool? It didn't to me. I was young, and had not the clarity of judgment that Rothenstein already had. Soames was quite five or six years older than either of us. Also – he had written a book. It was wonderful to have written a book.

If Rothenstein had not been there, I should have revered Soames. Even as it was, I respected him. And I was very near indeed to reverence when he said he had another book coming out soon. I asked if I might ask what kind of book it was.

'My poems,' he answered. Rothenstein asked if this was to be the title of the book. The poet meditated on this suggestion, but said he rather thought of giving the book no title at all. 'If a book is good in itself –' he murmured, and waved his cigarette.

★ ★ ★ ★ ★ ★ ★ ★ ★ ★ ★ ★

Not to buy a book of which I had met the author face to face would have been for me in those days an impossible act of self-denial. When I returned to Oxford for the Christmas term I had duly secured 'Negations'. I used to keep it lying carelessly on the table in my room, and whenever a friend took it up and asked what it was about, I would say: 'Oh, it's rather a remarkable book. It's by a man whom I know.' Just 'what it was about' I never was able to say. Head or tail was just what I hadn't made of that slim, green volume. I found in the preface no clue to the labyrinth of contents, and in that labyrinth nothing to explain the preface.

Lean near to life. Lean very near –
nearer.

Life is web and therein nor warp nor
woof is, but web only.

It is for this I am Catholick in church
and in thought, yet do let swift Mood weave
there what the shuttle of Mood wills.

These were the opening phrases of the preface, but those which followed were less easy to understand. Then came 'Stark: A Conte' about a midinette who, so far as I could gather, murdered, or was about to murder, a mannequin. It was rather like a story by Catulle Mendès in which the translator had either skipped or cut out every alternate sentence. Next, a dialogue between Pan and St. Ursula, lacking, I rather thought, in 'snap'. Next, some aphorisms (entitled [ ]). Throughout, in fact, there was a great variety of form, and the forms had evidently been wrought with much care. It was rather the substance that eluded me. Was there, I wondered, any substance at all? It did not occur to me: suppose Enoch Soames was a fool! Up cropped a rival hypothesis: suppose – I – was! I inclined to give Soames the benefit of the doubt. I had read 'L'Après-midi d'un faune' without extracting a glimmer of meaning; yet Mallarmé, of course, was a master. How was I to know that Soames wasn't another? There was a sort of music in his prose, not indeed, arresting, but perhaps, I thought, haunting, and laden, perhaps, with meanings as deep as Mallarmé's own. I awaited his poems with an open mind.

And I looked forward to them with positive impatience after I had a second meeting with him. This was on an evening in January. Going into the aforesaid domino-room, I had passed a table at which sat a pale man with an open book before him. He had looked from his book to me, and I looked back over my shoulder with a vague sense that I ought to have recognized him. I returned to pay my respects. After exchanging a few words, I said with a glance to the open book, 'I see I am interrupting you,' and was about to pass on, but, 'I prefer,' Soames replied in his toneless voice, 'to be interrupted,' and I obeyed his gesture that I should sit down.

I asked him if he often read there.

'Yes; things of this kind I read here,' he answered, indicating the title of his book – 'The Poems of Shelley'.

'Anything that you really' – and I was going to say 'admire?' But I cautiously left my sentence unfinished, and was glad that I had done so, for he said with unwonted emphasis, 'Anything second-rate.'

I had read little of Shelley, but, 'Of course,' I murmured, 'he's very uneven.'

'I should have thought evenness was just what was wrong with him. A deadly evenness. That's why I read him here. The noise of this place breaks the rhythm. He's tolerable here.' Soames took up the book and glanced through the pages. He laughed. Soames's laugh was a short, single, and mirthless sound from the throat, unaccompanied by any movement of the face or brightening of the eyes. 'What a period!' he uttered, laying the book down. And, 'What a country!' he added.

I asked him rather nervously if he didn't think Keats had more or less held his own against the drawbacks of time and place. He admitted that there were 'passages in Keats' but didn't specify them. Of 'the older men' as he called them, he seemed to like only Milton. 'Milton,' he said, 'wasn't sentimental.' Also, 'Milton had a dark insight.' And again, 'I can always read Milton in the reading-room.'

'The reading-room?'

'Of the British Museum. I go there every day.'

'You do? I've only been there once. I'm afraid I found it rather a depressing place. It – it seemed to sap one's vitality.'

'It does. That's why I go there. The lower one's vitality, the more sensitive one is to great art. I live near the museum. I have rooms in Dyott Street.'

'And you go round to the reading-room to read Milton?'

'Usually Milton.' He looked at me. 'It was Milton,' he certificatively added, 'who converted me to diabolism.'

'Diabolism? Oh, yes? Really?' said I, with that vague discomfort and that intense desire to be polite which one feels when a man speaks of his own religion. 'You – you worship the devil?'

Soames shook his head.

'It's not exactly worship,' he qualified, sipping his absinthe. 'It's more a matter of trusting and encouraging.'

## 40

## STELLA MARIS

*Arthur Symons*

Why is it I remember yet
You, of all women one has met
In random wayfare, as one meets
The chance romances of the streets,
The Juliet of a night? I know
Your heart holds many a Romeo.
And I, who call to mind your face
In so serene a pausing-place,
Where the bright pure expanse of sea,
The shadowy shore's austerity,
Seems a reproach to you and me,
I too have sought on many a breast
The ecstasy of love's unrest,
I too have had my dreams, and met
(Ah me!) how many a Juliet.
Why is it then, that I recall
You, neither first nor last of all
For, surely as I see to-night
The glancing of the lighthouse light,
Against the sky, across the bay,
As turn by turn it falls my way,
So surely do I see your eyes
Out of the empty night arise,
Child, you arise and smile to me
Out of the night, out of the sea,
The Nereid of a moment there,
And is it seaweed in your hair?

O lost and wrecked, how long ago,
Out of the drowned past, I know,
You come to call me, come to claim
My share of your delicious shame.

Child, I remember, and can tell
One night we loved each other well;
And one night's love, at least or most,
Is not so small a thing to boast.
You were adorable, and I
Adored you to infinity,
That nuptial night too briefly borne
To the oblivion of morn.
Oh, no oblivion! for I feel
Your lips deliriously steal
Along my neck, and fasten there;
I feel the perfume of your hair,
And your soft breast that heaves and dips,
Desiring my desirous lips,
And that ineffable delight
When souls turn bodies, and unite
In the intolerable, the whole
Rapture of the embodied soul.

That joy was ours, we passed it by;
You have forgotten me, and I
Remember you thus strangely, won
An instant from oblivion.
And I, remembering, would declare
That joy, not shame, is ours to share,
Joy that we had the will and power,
In spite of fate, to snatch one hour,
Out of vague nights, and days at strife,
So infinitely full of life.
And 'tis for this I see you rise,
A wraith, with starlight in your eyes,
Here, where the drowsy-minded mood
Is one with Nature's solitude;
For this, for this, you come to me
Out of the night, out of the sea.

## 41

## ORCHIDS

*Theodore Wratislaw*

Orange and purple, shot with white and mauve,
Such in a greenhouse wet with tropic heat
One sees these delicate flowers whose parents throve
In some Pacific island's hot retreat.

Their ardent colours that betray the rank
Fierce hotbed of corruption whence they rose
Please eyes that long for stranger sweets than prank
Wild meadow-blooms and what the garden shows.

Exotic flowers! How great is my delight
To watch your petals curiously wrought,
To lie among your splendours day and night
Lost in a subtle dream of subtler thought.

Bathed in your clamorous orchestra of hues,
The palette of your perfumes, let me sleep
While your mesmeric presences diffuse
Weird dreams; and then bizarre sweet rhymes shall creep

Forth from my brain and slowly form and make
Sweet poems as a spider weaving spins,
A shrine of loves that laugh and swoon and ache,
A temple of coloured sorrows and perfumed sins!

## 42

# Passages from THE STORY OF VENUS AND TANNHAUSER

*Aubrey Beardsley*

from Chapter I

The Chevalier Tannhauser, having lighted off his horse, stood doubtfully for a moment beneath the ombre gateway of the Venusberg, troubled with an exquisite fear lest a day's travel should have too cruelly undone the laboured niceness of his dress. His hand, slim and gracious as the Marquise du Deffand's in the drawing by Carmontelle, played nervously about the gold hair that fell upon his shoulders like a finely curled peruke, and from point to point of a precise toilet, the fingers wandered, quelling the little mutinies of cravat and ruffle.

It was taper-time; when the tired earth puts on its cloak of mists and shadows, when the enchanted woods are stirred with light footfalls and slender voices of the fairies, when all the air is full of delicate influences, and even the beaux, seated at their dressing-tables, dream a little.

A delicious moment, thought Tannhauser, to slip into exile.

★ ★ ★ ★ ★ ★ ★ ★ ★ ★ ★ ★

from Chapter IX

The breakfasters were scattered over the gardens in têtes-a-têtes and tiny parties. Venus and Tannhauser sat together upon the lawn that lay in front of the Casino, and made havoc of a ravishing dejeuner. The Chevalier was feeling very happy. Everything around him seemed so white and light and matinal; the floating frocks of the ladies, the scarce robed boys and satyrs stepping hither and thither elegantly, with meats and wines and fruits; the damask tablecloths, the delicate talk and laughter that rose everywhere; the flowers' colour and the flowers' scent; the shady trees, the wind's cool voice, and the sky above that was as fresh and pastoral as a perfect fifth. And Venus looked so beautiful. Not at all like the lady in Lempriere.

'You're such a dear!' murmured Tannhauser, holding her hand.

At the further end of the lawn, and a little hidden by a rose-tree, a young man was breakfasting alone. He toyed nervously with his food now and then, but for the most part leant back in his chair with unemployed hands, and gazed stupidly at Venus.

'That's Felix,' said the Goddess, in answer to an enquiry from the Chevalier; and she went on to explain his attitude. Felix always attended Venus upon her little latrinal excursions, holding her, serving her, and making much of all she did. To undo her things, lift her skirts, to wait and watch the coming, to dip a lip or finger in the royal output, to stain himself deliciously with it, to lie beneath her as the favours fell, to carry off the crumped, crotted paper – these were the pleasures of that young man's life.

Truly there never was a queen so beloved by her subjects as Venus. Everything she wore had its lover. Heavens! how her handkerchiefs were filched, her stockings stolen! Daily, what intrigues, what countless ruses to possess her merest frippery! Every scrap of her body was adored. Never, for Savaral, could her ear yield sufficient wax! Never, for Pradon, could she spit prodigally enough! And Saphius found a month an interminable time.

After breakfast was over, and Felix's fears lest Tannhauser should have robbed him of his capricious rights had been dispelled, Venus invited the Chevalier to take a more extensive view of the gardens, parks, pavilions, and ornamental waters. The carriage was ordered. It was a delicate, shell-like affair, with billowy cushions and a light canopy, and was drawn by ten satyrs, dressed as finely as the coachmen of the Empress Pauline the First.

The drive proved interesting and various, and Tannhauser was quite delighted with almost everything he saw.

And who is not pleased when on either side of him rich lawns are spread with lovely frocks and white limbs, – and upon flowerbeds the dearest ladies are implicated in a glory of underclothing, – when he can see in the deep cool shadow of the trees warm boys entwined, here at the base, there in the branch, – when in the fountain's wave Love holds his court, and the insistent water burrows in every delicious crease and crevice?

A pretty sight, too, was little Rosalie, perched like a postilion upon the painted phallus of the gold of all gardens. Her eyes were closed and she was smiling as the carriage passed. Round her neck and slender girlish shoulders there was a cloud of complex dress, over which bulged her wig-like flaxen tresses. Her legs and feet were bare, and the toes twisted in an amorous style. At the foot of the statue lay her shoes and stockings and a few other things.

Tannhauser was singularly moved at this spectacle, and rose out of all proportion. Venus slipped the fingers of comfort under the lace flounces of his trousers, saying, 'Is it all mine? Is it all mine?' and doing fascinating things. In the end, the carriage was only prevented from being overturned by the happy intervention of Priapusa, who stepped out from somewhere or other just in time to preserve its balance.

How the old lady's eye glistened as Tannhauser withdrew his panting blade! In her sincere admiration for fine things, she quite forgot and forgave the shock she had received from the falling of the gay equipage. Venus and Tannhauser were profuse with apology and thanks, and quite a crowd of loving courtiers gathered round, consoling and congratulating in a breath.

The Chevalier vowed he never would go in the carriage again, and was really quite upset by it. However, after he had had a little support from the smelling-salts, he recovered his self-possession, and consented to drive on further.

The landscape grew rather mysterious. The park, no longer troubled and adorned with figures, was full of grey echoes and mysterious sounds; the leaves whispered a little sadly, and there was a grotto that murmured like the voice that haunts the silence of a deserted oracle. Tannhauser became a little triste. In the distance, through the trees, gleamed a still, argent lake – a reticent, romantic water that must have held the subtlest fish that ever were. Around its marge the tress and flags and fleurs de luce were unbreakably asleep.

The Chevalier fell into a strange mood, as he looked at the lake. It seemed to him that the thing would speak, reveal some curious secret, say some beautiful word, if he should dare wrinkle its pale face with a pebble.

'I should be frightened to do that, though,' he said to himself. Then he wondered what there might be upon the other side; other gardens, other gods? A thousand drowsy fancies passed through his brain. Sometimes the lake took fantastic shapes, or grew to twenty times its size, or shrunk into a miniature of itself, without ever once losing its unruffled calm, its deathly reserve. When the water increased, the Chevalier was very frightened, for he thought how huge the frogs must have become. He thought of their big eyes and monstrous wet feet, but when the water lessened he laughed to himself, whilst thinking how tiny the frogs must have grown. He thought of their legs that must look thinner than spiders', and of their dwindling croaking that never could be heard. Perhaps the lake was only painted, after all. He had seen things like it at the theatre. Anyhow, it was a wonderful lake, a beautiful lake, and he would love to bathe in it, but he was sure he would be drowned if he did.

## 43

## THE BARBER

*John Gray*

1

I dreamed I was a barber; and there went
Beneath my hand, oh! manes extravagant.
Beneath my trembling fingers, many a mask
Of many a pleasant girl. It was my task
To gild their hair, carefully, strand by strand;
To paint their eyebrows with a timid hand;
To draw a bodkin, from a vase of kohl,
Through the closed lashes; pencils from a bowl
Of sepia to paint them underneath;
To blow upon their eyes with a soft breath.
Then lay them back and watched the leaping bands.

2

The dream grew vague. I moulded with my hands
The mobile breasts, the valley; and the waist
I touched; and pigments reverently placed
Upon their thighs in sapient spots and stains,
Beryls and crysolites and diaphanes,
And gems whose hot harsh names are never said.
I was a masseur; and my fingers bled
With wonder as I touched their awful limbs.

3

Suddenly, in the marble trough, there seems
O, last of my pale mistresses, Sweetness!
A twylipped scarlet pansie. My caress

Tinges thy steelgray eyes to violet.
Adown thy body skips the pit-a-pat
Of treatment once heard in a hospital
For plagues that fascinate, but half appal.

4

So, at the sound, the blood of me stood cold.
Thy chaste hair ripened into sullen gold.
The throat, the shoulders, swelled and were uncouth.
The breasts rose up and offered each a mouth.
And on the belly pallid blushes crept,
That maddened me, until I laughed and wept.

44

## THE DESTROYER OF A SOUL

***John Davidson***

I hate you with a necessary hate.
First, I sought patience: passionate was she:
My patience turned in very scorn of me,
That I should dare forgive a sin so great,
As this, through which I sit disconsolate;
Mourning for that live soul, I used to see;
Soul of a saint, whose friend I used to be:
Till you came by! a cold, corrupting, fate.

Why come you now? You, whom I cannot cease
With pure and perfect hate to hate? Go, ring
The death-bell with a deep, triumphant toll!
Say you, my friend sits by me still? Ah, peace!
Call you this thing my friend? this nameless thing?
This living body, hiding its dead soul?

## 45

## LUCRETIA

***James Elroy Flecker***

*As one who in the cold abyss of night*
*Stares at a book whose grey print meaningless*
*Dances between the lamplight and his eyes,*
*Lucretius lay, soul-poisoned, conquering still*
*With towering travail Reason's Hellene heights.*
*Listen, Lucretia, to the voice of his pain:*

Thrice welcome hour of Reason: ne'er of old
Knew I thy naked loveliness, till night,
The nether night of Folly pinioned forth,
Shrouded my senses, taught me terribly
That thou alone, my light and life and love,
Wearest the high insignia of the stars.
Grant then thy worshipper, austerest Queen,
Refreshing dews – Now, now, I thirst with flame:
They flee the strainings of my fevered lips
Cruelly, and in dank distance a new noise
Of rushing wings I hear. Who thunders nigh?
Devil delirium, chaos charioted,
Curb, curb, the coal-red chargers, heard not seen.
See, Madam Wife, that loveless lust of thine
Leaves no sweet savour lingering, but a curse:
And 'stead of Love and Reason, palace tenant,
There flits a weak and tremulous loathsomeness!

*Suppliant fled Lucretia to the couch:*
*And all her glory trembled as she sang;*

Awake, dead soul of dear Lucretius,
Awake, thy witless fond destroyer prays.
Awake, awake, and quit thy aimless journey
In cold oblivion's purple-misted paths.

Dost thou remember, husband? It was evening:
We wandered shorewards, mid the ocean of air
That glassed the gliding Nereids of the Pole.
Immeasurable moonlight kissed the brow
Of the white sea whose ripples swayed to greet
Our heart's unnumbered laughter. Strongest sleep
So held the life of earth that dimly we heard
Time's fatal pulse through the dark reverberated.
Then died thy soul: that night I, murderess, dreamt,
Ah, dolorous dreams of limb-dissolving love.
Lucretius,
Why live I still, protracting hopeless pain?
The chillness of the long Lethean stream
Is more to be commended for my sailings
Than love's hot eddies.
God, for the draught of death!
What sourer, sweeter vintage could be pressed?
To slumber shall I lull me, where no sorrow
Can pierce the drifted overmantling haze:
No sorrow, no despair, nor any love!

My soul is thine, husband, thy mad soul.
Madness, swift foretaste of oblivion
Shall wed us to delirious dim despair
Till bone claim bone beneath the cypress tree.
What pleasant dawn of madness! Off I rend
This fair hypocrisy of raiment. Down –
There's fairer guile within – down, frippery!
Veil me not from my love. Dear arms outstretched,
Am I not fair? These quick white limbs of mine
Shall brand in thee their passionate symmetry,
Till as the bee within the lily trembles
Thyself, body and soul, shall move within me.
Has sculptured Venus thighs of richer vein?
Spread thyself round about me; let us wrench
Self unto self. Why life is lovely still!
Fair wings of madness, drift us far away
To an unseen Empyrean, where no care

Can frost the magic mirror of our loves.
Thence we shall see the sorrowful world of men,
Old castles fired, old mountains overturned,
Old majesties conculcate in the dust,
With short sad smiles for every thing destroyed.
Why do red eyes draw nearer? Husband, wake!
The palace is fired and falling! Not with love
Thy body's life, that throbs within me, burns
Lucretius – those same eyes, grey Furies wear them,
They seethe in double dullness 'neath their own!

*Thus muttered she in dread: he glaring lay:*
*Passion had made him beast, and passion sated*
*Did leave him than the beasts more bestial.*
*Till phantomed reason fled his turning brain*
*And with a cry he struck her from his breast,*
*Heavily, and her hair, like the finger of night,*
*Pencilled the marble as she fell, and cried;*

Kill me not, devil: off, blood-searching hands;
Nay, strike me thus – and rend me thus, and thus:
I would not be the mother of mad children.
Burst forth, my blood, burst forth from wound and
well
The body's pain is blister for the soul's.

*Then, as her anguish slumbered for awhile:*

Oh for a word of consolation dear
Sadder than dirge from old Simonides,
Sweeter than echoes of the Linos song
Whispering through the drowsy sheaves of corn
On summer evenings, when the harvesters
Homeward return, and children rush to greet
Their father, and to snatch the kisses first –

*But a new torment rent her, and she rose;*
*Her veins large-knotted, standing out in fire;*

*She grasped his arm and shrieked to the solemn sun*
*That rolled in horror down the Western Sea:*

There, red-eyed Fury – with lash and terrible hiss,
With lash and terrible hiss of steaming snakes –
Blood from the breast-wound drips, and from my heart,
And from those eyes, and from the pillars – See
There, and the statues move. Take away the blank eyes!
Oh wild, wild irony of Life and Lust,
Life is to death so near, and lust to loathing.
All is a jest, a shadow, and a lie.
A whirlwind-wondrous lie!
Laugh, husband, laugh!
Laughter is man's supreme prerogative:
The beasts are sane; they laugh not. I will laugh,
My bones and flesh are quaking. Laugh, thou fool!
For love is lust, and life is a dream of death
– Hell is opening, opening horribly.

## 46

## Extract from
## THE DEAD WALL
### *H. B. Marriott Watson*

The dawn stared raw and yellow out of the east at Rosewarne. Its bleak and ugly face smouldered through morose vapours. The wind blew sharp against the windows, shaking them in their casements. The prospect from that lonely chamber over-awed him with menace; it glowered upon him. The houses in the square, wrapped in immitigable doom, were to him ominous memorials of death. They frightened him into a formless panic. Anchored in that soundless sea, they terrified him with their very stillness. In dreary ranks they rose, a great high wall of doom, lifting their lank chimneys to the dreadful sky. They obsessed him with forebodings to which he could put no term, for which he could find no reason. Shrouded under its great terror, his poor mind fell into deeper depression under the influence of those malign and ugly signals. He strove to withdraw his thoughts and direct them upon some different subject. He wrenched them round to the contemplation of his room, his walls, his wife. A dull pain throbbed in the back of his head. He repeated aloud the topics upon which he would have his mind revolve, but the words rang in his ears without meaning. He touched the pictures on the wall, he spoke their names, he covered his face and strained hard to recapture coherent thought. The subjects mocked him: they were too nimble and elusive for his tired brain; they danced out of reach, and he followed blindly till a deeper darkness fell. They grew faint and shadowy, like wraiths in a mist, and he pursued the glancing shadows. Finally, his brain grew blank; it was as if consciousness had lapsed; and he found himself regarding a fly that crawled upon the pane. Outside lay the oppression of that appalling scene that horrified him – he knew not why.

Rosewarne was growing used to these nervous exhibitions. This unequal struggle had been repeated through many weeks, but he had always so far come out of it with personal security. The dread that some day he would fail continually haunted him, and increased the strain of the conflict. He wondered what lay at the back of this horrible condition, and shuddered as he wondered. And he knew now that he must not let himself adrift, but must dispose the devils by every means. He broke into a whistle, and moved about the room carelessly. It was a lively stave from the streets that his lips framed, but it conveyed to him no sense of sound. He perambulated the chamber with a false air of cheerfulness. He eyed the bed with his head askew, winking as if to share a jest with it. He patted the pillows, arranging them and disarranging them in turn. He laughed softly, merrily, emptily. He seized the dumb-bells from the mantelpiece and whirled them about his head; he chafed his hands, he rubbed his flesh. Little by little the blood moved with more content through his body, and the pulse of his heart sank slowly.

Outside, the dawn brightened and the wind came faster. Rosewarne looked forth and nodded; then he turned and left the room, his face flashing as he passed the mirror, like the distempered face of a corpse. Across the landing he paused before a door, and, bending to the keyhole, listened; little low sounds of life came to his ears, and suddenly his haggard face crowded with emotions. He rose and softly descended the stairs to his study. The house lay in the quiet of sleep, and within the solitude of that rich room, he, too, was as still as the sleepers. The inferior parts of the window formed a blind of stained glass, but the grey light flowed through the upper panes into a magnificent wilderness. The cold ashes of the fire, by which he had sat at his task late into the morning, lay still within the grate. The little ensigns of a human presence, the scattered papers, the dirty hearth, all the instruments of his work, looked mean and squalid within the spacious dignity of that high room. He lit the gas and sat down to his table, moving his restless fingers among the papers. It was as if his members arrogantly claimed their independence, and refused the commands of a weak brain. His mind had abrogated. His hands shifted furtively like the hands of a pickpocket: they wandered among the papers and returned to him. The clock droned out the hour slowly, and that he started, shook his wits together, and began in haste to turn about the documents. He knew now the sheet of which he had sent his hands in quest. Large and blue and awful, it had been his ghost throughout the night. He could see the figures scrawled upon it in his own tremulous handwriting, rows upon rows of them, thin and sparse and self-respecting at the top, but to the close, fevered, misshapen, and reckless, fighting and jostling in a crowd for space upon the page. He laid his hand upon the horrible thing; he opened his ledgers; and sat deciphering once more his own ruin.

The tragedy lay bare to his shrinking eyes; it leaped forth at him from the blurred and confused figures. There was no need to rehearse them; he had reiterated them upon a hundred scrolls in a hundred various ways these many weeks. They had become his enemies, to deceive whom he had invoked the wreck of a fine intelligence. He had used all the wiles and dodges of a cunning mind to entrap them to his service. He had spent a weary campaign upon them, storming them with fresh troops of figures, deploying and ambuscading with all the subterfuge of a subtle business mind. But there now, as at the outset of his hopeless fight, the issue remained unchanged; the terrible sum of his sin abided, unsubtracted, undivided, unabridged. As he regarded it at this moment it seemed to assume quickly a vaster proportion. His crime cried out upon him, calling for vengeance in his ears. Seizing a pen, eagerly, vacantly, he set forth anew to recompose the items.

Rosewarne worked on for a couple of hours, holding his quivering fingers to the paper by the sheer remnants of his will. His brain refused its offices, and he stumbled among the numerical problems with false and blundering steps. To add one sum to another he must ransack the litter of his mind; the knowledge that runs glibly to the tongue of a child he must rediscover by a persistent and arduous concentration. But still he kept his seat, and jotted down his cyphers. About him the house stirred slowly; noises passed his door and faded; the grim and yellow sun rose higher and struck upon the table, contending with the gaslight. But Rosewarne paid no heed; he wrestled with his numb brain and his shivering fingers, wrestled to the close of the page; where once more the hateful figures gleamed in bold ink, menacing and blinking, his old ghost renewed and invested with fresh life.

The pen dropped from his hand, his head fell upon his arms, and as he lay in that helpless attitude of despair that protests not, of misery that can make no appeal, the door fell softly open and his wife entered.

## 47

## PASSION

*Richard Garnett*

This flame of Passion that so high in air,
   By spice and balsam of the spirit fed,
   With fire and fume vast Heaven hath overspread,
And blots the stars with smoke, or dims with glare:
Soon shall it droop, and radiance pure and fair
   Again from azure altitudes be shed;
   And we the murky grime and embers red
Shall sift, if haply dust of Love be there.
Gather his ashes from the torrid mould,
   And, quenched with drops of Bacchic revelry,
   Yield to the Stygian powers to have and hold:
And urn Etrurian let his coffin be;
   For this was made to store the dead and cold,
   And is a thing of much fragility.

## 48

## AGAINST MY LADY BURTON: ON HER BURNING THE LAST WRITING OF HER DEAD HUSBAND

***Ernest Dowson***

'To save his soul', whom narrowly she loved
She did this deed of everlasting shame,
For devils' laughter; and was soulless proved
Heaping dishonour on her scholar's name.
Her lean distrust awoke when he was dead;
Dead, hardly cold; whose life was worn away
In scholarship's high service; from his head
She lightly tore his ultimate crown of bay.
His masterpiece, the ripe fruit of his age,
In art's despite she gave the hungry flame;
Smiled at the death of each laborious page,
Which she read only by the light of shame.
Dying he trusted her: him dead she paid
Most womanly, destroying his life's prize:
So Judas decently his Lord betrayed
With deep dishonour wrought in love's disguise.
With deep dishonour, for her jealous heart
His whole life's work, with light excuse put by
For love of him, or haply, hating art.
Oh Love be this, let us curse Love and die.
Nay! Love forgive: could such a craven thing
Love anywhere? but let her name pass down
Dishonoured through the ages, who did fling
To the rank scented mob a sage's crown,
And offered Fame, Love, Honour, mincingly
To her one God – sterile Propriety!

## 49

## IN BOHEMIA

*Arthur Symons*

Drawn blinds and flaring gas within,
   And wine, and women, and cigars;
Without, the city's heedless din;
   Above, the white unheeding stars.

And we, alike from each remote,
   The world that works, the heaven that waits,
Con our brief pleasures o'er by rote,
   The favourite pastime of the Fates.

We smoke, to fancy that we dream,
   And drink, a moment's joy to prove,
And fain would love, and only seem
   To love because we cannot love.

Draw back the blinds, put out the light:
   'Tis morning, let the daylight come.
God! how the women's cheeks are white,
   And how the sunlight strikes us dumb!

# APPENDIX:
# ENGLISH DECADENCE ELSEWHERE

This volume provides just a sample of English decadence: there are a great many more strange and interesting things to explore from other sources. Sadly, some texts are out of print, or are available only as expensive imports and antiquarian editions; libraries and second-hand bookshops remain the best resources. The internet comes into its own here, providing instantly printable copy of a good deal of decadent writing. It is worth looking at the sites of other genres as well, as authors like M. P. Shiel and R. Murray Gilchrist are now celebrated as classic detective-fiction and horror writers; in modern times Michael Moorcock's *Dancer at the End of Time* trilogy is an homage to the decadents of the 1890s. This appendix makes no claims to completeness: it suggests only a few avenues for further exploration.

## Writers

**Aubrey Beardsley (1872–1898)**
*The Story of Venus and Tannhauser*, also known as *Under the Hill*, represents his crowning literary achievement, despite remaining unfinished. Three poems, 'Carmen CI', 'The Three Musicians' and 'The Ballad of a Barber', originally published in *The Savoy*, represent virtually all his published verse output. The literary works are not readily available, despite his fame: some period anthologies hold the poems; scouring the internet is necessary for *Venus and Tannhauser*. These are good, contemporary biographies: *Aubrey Beardsley: At the Sign of the Unicorn* (1898) by Arthur Symons, and *Aubrey Beardsley* (1909) by Robert Ross. Later: *Aubrey Beardsley: The Man and his Work* (1928) by Haldane Macfall.

**William Beckford (1760–1844)**

Brian Fothergill's *Beckford of Fonthill* (1979) is an authority which doesn't shy from frankness in detailing the overlooked godfather of English decadence's exploits and interests. Beckford's other writings of pertinence include *The Vision* (or, 'The Long Story', 1777). The availability of works other than *Vathek*-related material is not good, however; have a look at the superbly furnished Beckfordiana site at http://beckford.c18.net, which houses absolutely everything.

**Thomas Lovell Beddoes (1803–1849)**

*Death's Jest-Book, or The Fool's Tragedy* (1850) was left unfinished and unpublished when Beddoes finally poisoned himself after several unsuccessful attempts. It is a cocktail of bizarre, gothic grotesquery, and a piquant valentine to the black humour and bloodshed of the Elizabethan and Jacobean dramatists.

**Sir Max Beerbohm (1872–1956)**

Now here is a man who never took things too seriously. *The Works of Max Beerbohm* (1896) included some great essays, such as '1880', with *More* (1899) later. He lived far too long to list everything of note, but the Oxford novel *Zuleika Dobson* (1911) is richly frivolous and brilliantly written.

**George Gordon, Lord Byron (1788–1824)**

Benita Eisler's *Child of Passion, Fool of Fame* (1999) is as encyclopaedic as it is sensational and fascinating. Contemporary portraits include former lover Lady Caroline Lamb's *Glenarvon* (1816), and *The Vampyre* (1819), by Dr. John Polidori, his physician and sometime companion. Also, Edward John Trelawny added to the myth with his *Recollections of the Last Days of Shelley and Byron* (1858): he knew them both, but was also fond of storytelling. Thomas Moore, another friend, apparently salvaged some of the burned manuscripts of Byron's 'scandalous' diaries and edited them into *Letters and Journals of Lord Byron* (1830). The poet's grandson, Ralph Milbanke, wrote to vindicate his grandmother with *Astarte: A Fragment of Truth Concerning George Gordon Byron, Sixth Lord Byron*, a 1905 edition of which is currently available for $350 online. It is easy to track down on the internet Byron's 'Fragment of a Novel' (1816), the unfinished vampire story emerging from the night of June 18, 1816, which also gave the world Mary Shelley and *Frankenstein*. Finally, see the lavish www.byronmania.com

**William Cowper (1731–1800)**
Cowper lived his life subjected to periodic bouts of insanity which ultimately convinced him that he had been elected for damnation. He wrote throughout all this, and, though his poems are not decadent in subject matter, *The Task* (1785) in particular shares the intensity, absurdity and perverse humour of decadence.

**John Davidson (1857–1909)**
*In a Music-Hall* (1891) and *Fleet Street Eclogues* (1893) achieved some popularity, but after that a bitterness, and Nietzsche, set in. Collections are generally available from libraries and second-hand.

**Thomas De Quincey (1785–1859)**
*Confessions of an English Opium-Eater* was first published in 1821; by 1855 De Quincey was expanding and revising the work for a new edition of his writings. Both versions are currently available, but De Quincey himself had doubts as to whether he had actually made any improvements with his expansions, so *caveat emptor*. Otherwise, Grevel Lindop's *The Opium-Eater: A Life of Thomas De Quincey* (1981) remains the best biography.

**Lord Alfred Douglas (1870–1945)**
The author, and not the poetry, has a place in literary history, but his writing was done in the most appropriate atmosphere imaginable. Audio recordings of Bosie reading his poems were exhibited at the British Library 2000–2001, as part of a Wilde centenary. In his own, firm words: *The Autobiography of*

*Lord Alfred Douglas* (1929). *Bosie: A Biography of Lord Alfred Douglas* (2000) by Douglas Murray is the most recent biography, written whilst the author was a 20 year-old student at Oxford.

**Ernest Dowson (1867–1900)**
*Verses* (1896), *The Pierrot of the Minute* (1897) and *Decorations* (1899). He also wrote some short stories, which are generally overlooked: 'Apple Blossom', 'The Diary of a Successful Man', 'A Case of Conscience', 'An Orchestral Violin', 'Souvenirs of an Egoist', 'The Statue of Limitations', 'The Dying of Francis Donne'. See also some prose poems: 'Absinthia Taetra', 'The Visit'. Two novels, *A Dance of Masks* (1893) and *Adrian Rome* (1899), both written with Arthur Moore, seem to have vanished. However, *Madder Music, Stronger Wine: The Life of Ernest Dowson, Poet and Decadent* (2000) by Jad Adams is a welcome, modern appreciation of the man.

**James Elroy Flecker (1884–1915)**
*Hassan* (1922) is what is most commonly available second-hand, and is perhaps his best known drama. The Oriental fascination in his writing is infectious, and other works of interest are *The Golden Journey to Samarkand* (1913) and *The King of Alsander* (1913).

**Richard Garnett (1835–1906)**
When Wilde was sentenced, Garnett proclaimed the death of British verse for the next fifty years. He worked as the editor of the British Museum Catalogue, and Supervisor of the Reading Room and Keeper of Printed Books, but in contributing to *The Yellow Book* and writing the exotic short-story collection *The Twilight of the Gods* (1888) he clearly yearned for much less respectability.

**Edward Gibbon (1737–1794)**
He spent twenty years writing the *Decline and Fall*, and had planned something similar for English history, but death intervened.

**Sir W. S. Gilbert (1836–1911)**
He worked with Sir Arthur Sullivan between 1871 and 1896, producing 14 operettas, including *The Mikado* (1885), and was the subject of a Mike Leigh film (see below). He was also a journalist, playwright and poet, and died trying to save a friend from drowning.

**John Gray (1866–1934)**
*Silverpoints* (1893): the classic 'slim' volume of decadence. Embraced Catholicism in 1890 which became his vocation, accepting a parish near Edinburgh.

**Felicia Dorothea Hemans (1793–1835)**
A prolific producer of historical, sentimental and patriotic verse, Hemans was far too industrious and successful to fall prey to decadence. However, 'Thoughts During Sickness' (1835) demonstrates the extent to which De Quincey and Coleridge had influenced poets in the mainstream.

**Lionel Johnson (1867–1902)**
*Poems* (1895) and *Ireland* (1897); 'The Cultured Faun' essay is highly entertaining to read: it was meant to be parodic, but the superb writing betrays the author's true affection for the genre.

**John Keats (1795–1821)**
Wrote 'That I might drink, and leave the world unseen,' in 'Ode to a Nightingale'. See all the Odes, 'Sleep and Poetry' (1817), and *Endymion* (1818?) for the language that invented decadence. This is the inscription on his grave: 'Here lies One Whose name was Writ in Water'. For a modern, masterfully written biography, Andrew Motion's *Keats* (1998) is the best.

**Richard Le Gallienne (1866–1947)**
*English Poems* (1892) holds 'The Decadent to His Soul' and a few others of interest, and is worth tracking down. *The Romantic Nineties* (1925): a Rhymer and friend to Wilde, these

memoirs offer vivid first-hand portraits and anecdotes unavailable anywhere else. Sadly, editions are relatively rare: try the reserve stock of a large, metropolitan library.

**Arthur Machen (1863–1947)**

*The Hill of Dreams* (1897) is a grand, hallucinatory and paranoiac vision of metropolitanism. Machen's work isn't necessarily decadent, but it was contemporary and its perversities are more than appropriate. *The Great God Pan* (1894) is thoroughly disturbing, and as such deserves to be read in full. His writing is readily available from libraries and online: see www.machensoc.demon.co.uk

**George Moore (1852–1933)**

*Evelyn Innes* (1898) is a romance of straightforward aesthetical sensualism: music and art replacing life and enthusiasm for French literature. Moore lived on well into the twentieth century, retaining an interest in antiquity's ideals, though the latter works never matched the swagger and brio of *Confessions of a Young Man* (1888). His works are readily available second-hand.

**Walter Pater (1839–1894)**

*Marius the Epicurean* (1885) is his great novel of aesthetic sensations and reflections; the sheer refinement of the writing renders it indispensable. In his *Autobiographies* W. B. Yeats wonders if this book 'had not caused the disasters of my friends.' See also *Imaginary Portraits* (1887) for some bizarre but beautifully written characters.

**Bryan Waller Procter ('Barry Cornwall') (1787–1874)**

Friend to Charles Lamb, Charles Dickens and radical publisher Leigh Hunt, Procter was both a London lawyer and a man of letters. 'A Dream' (1819) demonstrates the influence of the hallucinatory reveries made popular by Coleridge, and the Georgian vogue for Oriental fantasy.

**Dante Gabriel Rossetti (1828–1882)**
His poems are collected and readily available; like Keats, he was extremely sensitive to criticism, and the 'Fleshly School' backlash greatly diminished his confidence in his own poetical abilities.

**Percy Bysshe Shelley (1792–1822)**
The writer that first excited the decadent sensibilities of the young Algernon Charles Swinburne and George Moore. See 'Alastor; or, The Spirit of Solitude', 'Adonais; an Elegy on the Death of John Keats', 'Marianne's Dream', 'Stanzas Written in Dejection Near Naples', 'The Witch of Atlas' and the dark, fierce prose of 'The Assassins', all of which anticipate the decadent mode.

**Algernon Charles Swinburne (1837–1909)**
The *mal viveur par excellence*. A version of Maupassant's bizarre encounter with the poet was recounted in the preface to an 1891 French translation of *Poems and Ballads*. Swinburne's prose, though exquisitely crafted, is fragmentary, such as the unfinished, posthumously-published *Lesbia Brandon* (1952), or restrained and epistolary, as with *Love's Cross-Currents* (1905; though written in 1862 and published first in 1877 as *A Year's Letters*, by Mrs. Horace Manners). These are generally available on the internet or as imports.

**Arthur Symons (1865–1945)**
The following collections are essential decadent literature: *Days and Nights* (1889); *Silhouettes* (1896); *London Nights* (1895, 1897); also 'The Decadent Movement in Literature' essay (1893). His achievement for the twentieth century was to bring Symbolism to England, both in *The Symbolist Movement in Literature* (1899) and with his translations of Verlaine, Gautier *et. al.* that T. S. Eliot and Ezra Pound were so grateful for. See homepages.nildram.co.uk/˜simmers/symons.htm

**Alfred, Lord Tennyson (1809–1892)**
Tennyson remains the laureate of morbid eloquence. As with the Pre-Raphaelites, his sense of sound is exquisite and was clearly an influence on decadent writers; *Maud* is gorgeously gloomy, as is 'Mariana'.

**James Thomson (1834–1882)**
*The City of Dreadful Night* (1874). He was a chronic insomniac and alcoholic, which clearly informs the writing. His works are mostly out of print, but can be found sometimes in old anthologies.

**H. B. Marriott Watson (1863–1921)**
Australian-born writer who came to England and caught the mood of *The Yellow Book* well, although elsewhere his concerns are less relevant to decadence. His wife Rosamund also contributed to the quarterly, and her work is more readily available.

**Oscar Wilde (1854–1900)**
The avatar and martyr of all things decadent. Richard Ellmann's *Oscar Wilde* (1987) remains the regal biography, out of a great many. *Table Talk* (2000) is a superb collection of stories told in conversation, assembled from hard-to-find letters, memoirs and autobiographies. *Selected Journalism* (2004) contains some divertingly dandyish opinions on cuisine and dress. Wilde on the internet is a vast and variable safari, but one generally entertaining.

**Theodore Wratislaw (1871–1933)**
*Caprices* (1893) and *Orchids* (1896); also contributed to *The Yellow Book* and *The Savoy*. Considered of secondary interest, and rather derivative of Symons; available only in anthologies and in university libraries.

## Autobiography, Memoir and Contemporary Study

**Frank Harris (1856–1931)**
*Oscar Wilde: His Life and Confessions* (1916): this was written over a decade after Wilde's death, and contains many 'verbatim' conversations which have attracted criticism, as well as other inaccuracies of time and place. Still, Harris knew Wilde and the nineties, and it remains fascinating stuff. Texts based on the 1930 edition include the explicit 'Confessions of Lord Alfred Douglas' material, and Bernard Shaw's 'My Memories of Oscar Wilde'. *My Life and Loves* : the first volume of Harris's autobiography that scandalised the twenties was published privately in Paris in 1922, and with accompanying pictures of nude women.

**Laurence Housman (1865–1959)**
*Echoes de Paris* (1923) is his memoir of the capital of all things decadent, including Wilde's last years.

**Holbrook Jackson (1874–1948)**
*The Eighteen Nineties* (1913) is a great, in-depth study of the decade and recently reprinted by Tantallon Press.

**Robert Harborough Sherard (1861–1943)**
*Oscar Wilde: The Story of an Unhappy Friendship* (1902); *The Life of Oscar Wilde* (1906); *The Real Oscar Wilde* (1917); a novel: *A Bartered Honour* (1883); poetry: *Whispers* (1884): Robert Sherard was a friend to Oscar Wilde and to Ernest Dowson in his last days, who died in Sherard's house. He wrote chiefly as a journalist, and notably campaigned against child-labour. His works from the decadent period are difficult to track down, and are absolutely collectable.

**W. B. Yeats (1865–1939)**
The first volume of his *Autobiographies* appeared in 1916, 'The Tragic Generation' was published in 1922, and there have been numerous editions and collections of these powerful, first-hand accounts of the decadent nineties ever since.

## Artists and Artworks

**Aubrey Beardsley (1872–1898)**
Beerbohm referred to the 1890s as 'the Beardsley period.' The illustrator's working methods were suitably peculiar: he never used a model, and he drew only by candlelight, even in the daytime. Some illustrations, such as *The Toilet of Salome I* and *II* (both 1894) detail little libraries of decadence: *The Golden Ass* by Lucius Apuleius, *Manon Lescaut* by Abbé Prévost, *Fêtes Galantes* by Paul Verlaine, *Nana* by Émile Zola. After *The Savoy* much of his work was unpublishably erotic, even by Smithers' standards. His final efforts were with Gautier's *Mademoiselle De Maupin* and Jonson's *Volpone* and are breathtaking, regardless of the state of his health. For near-contemporary memoir: *The Sheltering Tree* (1939) by friend and *Yellow Book* contributor Netta Syrett; for critical study: *The Beardsley Period* (1925) by Osbert Burdett.

**Sir Max Beerbohm (1872–1956)**
Mercilessly caricatured anyone of note at the time. Originals of *Rossetti and His Circle* (1922) are held by the Tate Gallery.

**Laurence Housman (1865–1959)**
Friend to Wilde in days of Paris exile. The delightfully grotesque 1892 illustrations for Christina Rossetti's *Goblin Market* are his most celebrated works, and he occasionally assisted John Lane with the artwork for *The Yellow Book* after Beardsley's departure.

**John Everett Millais (1829–1896)**
*Ophelia* (1852): beauty and death.

**Dante Gabriel Rossetti (1828–1882)**
Maidens gape heavenward, but their ecstasies are of this world.

**Henry Wallis (1830–1916)**
*Chatterton* (1856): beauty and death again, and the perfect end for the decadent. Ruskin described this picture as 'faultless and wonderful.'

**James McNeill Whistler (1834–1903)**
The only wit that could compete with Wilde. These controversial paintings placed sense and sensation over verisimilitude:
*Nocturne in Blue and Gold: Old Battersea Bridge* (1872–77)
*Nocturne in Black and Gold: The Falling Rocket* (1875)

## Magazines, Journals and Periodicals

***The Chameleon***
One issue only in December, 1894, and edited by John Francis Bloxam whilst still a student at Exeter College, Oxford. Described in the press as 'an insult to the animal creation' it printed Wilde's 'Phrases and Philosophies for the use of the Young', Bloxam's anonymous short-story 'The Priest and the Acolyte' (disastrously attributed to Wilde at his trial), and two poems by Lord Alfred Douglas: 'In Praise of Shame' and the infamous 'Two Loves'. The latter ends with 'I am the love that dare not speak its name.' All the material is readily available online.

***The Dial***
Edited by artists Charles Ricketts (1866–1931), who also illustrated Wilde's *The Sphinx* (1894), and Charles Shannon (1863–1937); they published five irregular issues between 1889 and 1897. Contributors included John Gray and Michael Field; it also published some of the first Symbolist art in England. Sadly, it is much easier to get hold of books about Ricketts that contain material from *The Dial*, rather than any facsimiles or reprints.

***The Savoy***

There were eight volumes in all. Irish poet George Russell warned his friend Yeats against involvement with this 'Origin of the Incubi and Succubi'. There are websites and books on the hotel and D'Oyly Carte that mention the periodical, but it is easier to track down the content through the individual contributors: editors Beardsley and Symons, also Sir Max Beerbohm, Charles Conder, Joseph Conrad, Ernest Dowson, Havelock Ellis, Selwyn Image, Lionel Johnson, Charles Shannon and W. B. Yeats.

***The Woman's World***

There were twenty issues edited by Oscar Wilde between 1887 and 1889; he contributed the informative and entertaining 'Literary and Other Notes'. A piece by Arthur Symons on Villiers de l'Isle Adam somehow got through. Unsurprisingly, there is scant availability outside collections of Wilde's more peripheral writing.

***The Yellow Book***

There were thirteen volumes in all. Due to Beardsley's involvement, there are plenty of images in circulation of the quarterly, although as he was employed only for the first four issues these tend to be the most available facsimiles. As with *The Savoy*, its literary contents are easier to track down by the individual contributors. Anthologies are available in some university libraries. An original edition for sale online is available at the moment for $1,600.

## Others of Interest

**Thomas Carlyle (1795–1881)**

*The French Revolution* (1837) includes one of the first instances of the word 'decadence' in English. This is extravagant, 'imaginative' history that Wilde clearly approved of, as he could apparently recite entire passages at will.

**Samuel Taylor Coleridge (1772–1834)**
As with De Quincey, the young Coleridge took laudanum as a standard medical prescription, and then became the English model for the dissolute and visionary genius. 'Dejection: An Ode', 'The Wanderings of Cain', 'The Rime of the Ancient Mariner', 'Christabel', 'Kubla Khan', 'A Tombless Epitaph', 'The Visionary Hope' and 'Limbo' are the writings of a brain shuddering from guilt, nerves and addiction. William Hazlitt records how Coleridge walked always in a crooked fashion; Wordsworth was alarmed at how his friend would unexpectedly throw himself to the ground in agony.

**Marie Corelli (1855–1924)**
One of the most prolific and successful writers of the 1890s; *Wormwood* (1890) is a mammoth and frequently hysterical condemnation of the cult of the green fairy. It is also emphatically and amusingly francophobic, denouncing the 'morbidness of the modern French mind.'

**Charles Dickens (1812–1870)**
*The Mystery of Edwin Drood* (1870) was his last, unfinished work, and a 'sensation novel' in the vein of Wilkie Collins. The novel's metropolis is an ancient city of darkness, opium dens, squalor and murder, and just the kind of place the English decadent would wander in the early hours.

**Elagabalus, or Heliogabalus (A. D. 203 / 204?–222)**
In artwork: *The Roses of Heliogabalus* (1888) by Sir Laurence Alma-Tadema depicts the extraordinary ending of an imperial dinner party. See also Simeon Solomon's *Heliogabalus, High Priest of the Sun* (1886). In literature: *The Amazing Emperor Heliogabalus* (1911) by John Stuart Hay, a biography; *The Sun God* (1904), a novel by Arthur Westcott. A new edition of Antonin Artaud's play *Heliogabalus, or The Crowned Anarchist* (1934) is currently being reprinted. There is a wealth of material devoted to this extraordinary person on the internet, who even manages to feature on cookery sites that discuss his

absurdly extravagant culinary tastes. These included ostrich brains and camel dung.

**Ronald Firbank (1886–1926)**
His novels include *Valmouth* (1919); *Sorrow In Sunlight* (1924); *Concerning the Eccentricities of Cardinal Pirelli* (1926). Firbank's prose is elegant and often dizzyingly baroque, though he wrote too late to catch the morbidity of the 1890s, however.

**R. Murray Gilchrist (1868–1917)**
His early, major work of interest is *The Stone Dragon and Other Tragic Romances* (1894), a morbid and ornate phantasmagoria that has been appropriated by the horror genre. His writing is readily available in libraries and on horror sites.

**W. E. Henley (1849–1903)**
Identified by Arthur Symons in 'The Decadent Movement in Literature' as possessing a proto-decadent sensibility along with Walter Pater, although many of his works are far too optimistic to warrant too much interest. As editor of the *National Observer* he established a group of counter-decadents: writers of a more muscular literary mettle, such as Rudyard Kipling.

**Robert Hichens (1864–1950)**
In *The Green Carnation* (1894) the friendship between grand conversationalist Mr. Amarinth and callow Lord Reggie is unmistakable, and the Marquis of Queensberry was thoroughly unamused by it. The press thought Wilde the author, and he was sufficiently irritated to write to the editor of the *Pall Mall Gazette* to deny any association with this 'mediocre book that usurps its strangely beautiful name'.

**Eugene Lee-Hamilton (1845–1907)**
*The New Medusa* (1882), *Sonnets of the Wingless Hours* (1894). Long-term invalid and half-brother of Vernon Lee (Violet Paget), the writer of bizarre historical stories. Lee-Hamilton's writing is generally available in anthologies of the period and in university libraries.

**Charles Robert Maturin (1782–1824)**
In Continental exile, Wilde would check himself into hotels as one Sebastian Melmoth, a name appropriated from Guido Reni's painting *San Sebastian* and Charles Maturin's cursed anti-hero in *Melmoth the Wanderer* (1820).

**Max Nordau (1849–1923)**
*Degeneration* (1895) was supposed to be a righteous condemnation of the debilitating effects of decadence on modern European culture; today, the heated prose perversely affirms and even romanticises what Nordau tried to vilify.

**Vincent O'Sullivan (1868–1940)**
He wrote *Poems* (1896) and *The Houses of Sin* (1897) before travelling and then lecturing at Rennes University in France. He died poverty-stricken in Paris. Like Lee-Hamilton, he is considered of secondary interest, and so generally exists only in anthologies and in university libraries.

**Mario Praz (1896–1982)**
His masterpiece *The Romantic Agony* (1933) is utterly indispensable. Although largely concerned with European writing, it catalogues pretty much anything of any interest in the Gothic, Romantic and decadent canons, including a great many forgotten classics.

**Marc-André Raffalovich (1864–1934)**
His relevant works are *A Willing Exile* (1890); *The Thread and the Path* (1895) and *L'Affaire Oscar Wilde* (1895). Raffalovich came from a wealthy Russian Jewish family who emigrated to Paris in the 1860s, and in England he sought to establish his own *salon*. He was piqued by Wilde's barbed wit, though: in *A Willing Exile* Cyprian Brome is instantly recognisable as a certain playwright and dandy, and his circle is paraded as slavish, vain, and very, very affected.

**Fr. Rolfe / 'Baron Corvo' (1860–1913)**
*Stories Toto Told Me* (1898) is a collection of mythological stories steeped in Catholicism's heady, esoteric lexicon; some

were featured in *The Yellow Book*. *Hadrian the Seventh* (1904) is his masterpiece of baroque writing and has been recently reprinted. His other, more historical writings tend to veer into fantastical extremities and are generally more collectable than readable.

**M. P. Shiel (1865–1947)**
Shiel's 1890s work in the main retained the Orientalist perversities of the Georgians, particularly with *Shapes in the Fire* (1896). *Prince Zaleski* (1895) is a collection of detective stories for the decadent era; both works are readily available online and in libraries.

**Christopher Smart (1722–1771)**
Confined in 1756 in a lunatic asylum for seven years, where he wrote *A Song to David* and *Jubilate Agno*. Christianity both excited and soothed his insanity, and the bizarre religious poems he wrote remain utterly unique.

**Leonard Smithers (1861–1907)**
Corresponded with Captain Sir Richard Burton, translator of *The Arabian Nights*, which initiated his career as publisher of the unorthodox and pornographic. Also quite a bibliophile: some titles from his own personal library were bound in human skin. Instrumental in the publishing of decadent works: he brought out *The Ballad of Reading Gaol* in 1898 when nobody would touch Wilde, and bankrolled *The Savoy* and Beardsley. After the success and excess of the nineties he drank himself to destruction. For a great portrait of an instrumental figure, *Publisher to the Decadents* by James G. Nelson (2000) comes recommended.

**Count Stanislaus Eric Stenbock (1859–1895)**
W. B. Yeats described him as, 'Scholar, connoisseur, drunkard, poet, pervert, most charming of men.' *Love, Sleep and Dreams* (1881?), *Myrtle, Rue amd Cypress* (1883), *The Shadow of Death* (1893) are all collections of his poetry, and his only prose

published in his lifetime was *Studies of Death* (1894). There has been recent reprint interest in the count as a seminal homoerotic writer.

**William Wordsworth (1770–1850)**
Not a decadent writer by any stretch of the imagination, but *The Prelude: Book V*, ll.56–140 is an intense, hallucinatory encounter with an Easterner. It is very vivid, and makes you wonder what else he might have written like this.

## Music

**Richard Wagner (1813–1883)**
If there is one composer whose works can lay claim to a decadent sensibility, it is Wagner. *Tristan*, completed in 1859, sent the aesthetes of Europe into ecstasies for over half a century. Performances of his works introduced new and epic feats of staging, effects and lighting that intoxicated audiences unused to such spectacle. Beardsley in particular was a devotee: see *The Wagnerites* (1894) from *The Yellow Book*, and *Isolde* from *The Studio* (1895).

## Film

*Cabaret* (Bob Fosse, 1972); Liza Minelli, Michael York, Joel Grey. Pre-WWII Berlin and the Kit-Kat Club provide the decadent setting; romantic ideals are cut to pieces against the rise of the Nazis.

*Caligula* (Tinto Brass, 1979); Malcolm McDowell, Helen Mirren, Peter O'Toole and John Gielgud. This is a supremely lavish reproduction of antiquity and imperial lunacy, entirely worthy of its notoriety.

*Death In Venice* (Luchino Visconti, 1971); Dirk Bogarde. A masterpiece that shows the fatal, pathetic isolation of the decadent.

*Gothic* (Ken Russell, 1986); Gabriel Byrne, Julian Sands. A feast for the eyes; its hysteria magnificently romanticises the heady days and nights at Lord Byron's Swiss residence of 1816.

*Moulin Rouge!* (Baz Luhrmann, 2001); Nicole Kidman, Ewan McGregor. This is a superb spectacle for the senses; it is air-brushed, anodyne decadence, but it looks and sounds fantastic.

*Performance* (Donald Cammall, Nicolas Roeg, 1970); James Fox, Mick Jagger. Sharp-suited gangster Fox descends into the unusual in Jagger's decadent bedlam. Thoroughly unwholesome sensory derangement.

*Rowing With The Wind* (Gonzalo Suarez, 1987); Hugh Grant, Elizabeth Hurley. This was made for television, but sumptuous enough, and Grant is a devilishly arrogant Lord Byron.

*Salomé's Last Dance* (Ken Russell, 1988); Glenda Jackson, Stratford Johns. Centred around an unusual performance of Wilde's play, taking place at a London brothel in 1895.

*Topsy-Turvy* (Mike Leigh, 2000); Jim Broadbent, Arthur Corduner. Consummately furnished portrait of *The Mikado*'s first production in 1885; the attention to detail in reproducing the late Victorian period is astonishing, and highly entertaining.

*Velvet Goldmine* (Todd Haynes, 1998); Jonathan Rhys Meyers, Ewan McGregor. Ackowledgement of the debt that the extravagance and debauchery of 1970s glam-rock owed to Oscar Wilde.

*Wilde* (Brian Gilbert, 1997); Stephen Fry, Jude Law. Lavish, modern retelling of the fall from grace.

## The Internet

**The 1890s Society**
www.1890s.org
This site provides a forum for discussion, links and new publications concerning the period. The society welcomes new members, and its interiors are supremely elegant.

**Project Gutenberg**
promo.net/pg
This is a vast, ever-expanding archive of texts available to print. Holds poetical works and some prose by Ernest Dowson, stories by Vernon Lee, and a lot more besides.

**The Victorian Web**
www.victorianweb.org
Superb overviews of anyone of any note in the Victorian age, with some texts available online, artwork, biography, and bibliography; also has pages devoted exclusively to aesthetes and decadents.

## Decadence from Dedalus

*Dedalus is "the premier publisher of decadent, turn-of-the-last-century European fiction." Michael Dirda in The Washington Post.*

*Titles available include:*

| Title | ISBN | Price |
|---|---|---|
| *Episodes of Vathek* Beckford | 1 873982 61 5 | £6.99 |
| *Senso (and other stories)* Boito | 0 946626 83 9 | £6.99 |
| *The Victim (L'Innocente)* D'Annunzio | 0 946626 64 2 | £7.99 |
| *Les Diaboliques* D'Aurevilly | 1 873982 27 5 | £7.99 |
| *Angels of Perversity* de Gourmont | 0 946626 72 3 | £6.99 |
| *Dedalus Book of Roman Decadence* Farrington | 1 873982 16 X | £8.99 |
| *Dedalus Book of German Decadence* Furness | 1 873982 21 6 | £9.99 |
| *Là-Bas* Huysmans | 1 873982 74 4 | £7.99 |
| *The Road to Darkness* Leppin | 1 873982 33 X | £7.99 |
| *Monsieur de Phocas* Lorrain | 1 873982 15 1 | £8.99 |
| *Abbé Jules* Mirbeau | 1 873982 37 2 | £8.99 |
| *The Diary of a Chambermaid* Mirbeau | 0 946626 82 0 | £7.99 |
| *Le Calvaire* Mirbeau | 0 946626 99 5 | £7.99 |
| *Sebastien Roch* Mirbeau | 1 873982 43 7 | £9.99 |
| *Torture Garden* Mirbeau | 1 873982 53 4 | £7.99 |
| *Monsieur Venus* Rachilde | 1 873982 20 8 | £6.99 |
| *La Marquise de Sade* Rachilde | 1 873982 06 2 | £8.99 |
| *The Great Shadow* Sà-Carneiro | 1 873982 72 0 | £8.99 |
| *Lucio's Confessions* Sà-Carneiro | 1 873982 80 1 | £6.99 |
| *Dedalus Book of Decadence* Stableford | 1 873982 01 1 | £7.99 |
| *Second Dedalus Book of Decadence* Stableford | 0 946626 80 4 | £8.99 |
| *Autumn & Winter Sonatas* Valle-Inclan | 1 873982 83 6 | £7.99 |
| *Spring & Summer Sonatas* Valle-Inclan | 1 873982 03 8 | £7.99 |
| *Dedalus Book of English Decadence* Willsher | 1 903517 26 5 | £8.99 |

**The Dedalus Book of Absinthe – Phil Baker**

"This is the sort of book it would be very easy to do badly. Phil Baker has, instead, done a magnificent job; it is formidably researched, beautifully written, and abundant with telling detail and pitch-black humour"

*Sam Leith in The Daily Telegraph*

"As to whether absinthe is harmful or this book irresponsible – I don't give a damn. All I know is that the former is very pleasant and the book is informative, amusingly written and perceptive. As the Idler put it a couple of years ago; tonight we're gonna party like its 1899."

*Nicholas Lezard, Guardian Pick of the Week*

"James Joyce in *Finnegan's Wake* described a character as 'absintheminded', while lesser punsters spoke of absinthe making ' the tart grow fonder'. It reaches across time, this 'potent concoction of eccentricity and beauty'. Alluring, then informative and witty."

*Brian Case, Time Out*

"hugely entertaining . . . excellent . . . merits prolonged and repeated consumption."

*Chris Hirst in The Independent*

"For someone who actually likes the beastly stuff, Phil Baker writes very well and drily . . . I greatly recommend the tasting notes of current brands at the end . . ."

*Philip Hensher in The Spectator*

"This is all great stuff, and sets us up for the extended coda of the modern absinthe. One of the most fascinating themes in this witty, erudite and desperately poignant study is that of the cultural war waged between England and France at the end of the 19th century. English moralists would wax not very eloquent on the sapping effects of absinthe on the susceptible French soul, always uncomfortably aware that the French were producing writers and artists of a calibre unmatched in England."

*Murrough O'Brien in the Independent on Sunday*

£9.99 ISBN 1 873982 94 1 296p B. Format

**The Dedalus Book of the Occult- Gary Lachman**

"Lachman's highly enjoyable survey makes lots of good points and all the right connections."

*Suzi Feay in The Independent on Sunday*

"Brisk, workmanlike and lucid, this is a survey of ' adventurous souls' whose output was the reverse: 'often crazy, sometimes hilarious and, on occasion, clearly insane'. Lachman's gallery of occultists ranges from the hypnotist Mesmer (1734–1815), whose salon had 'an orgy-like atmosphere', through Goethe and Balzac (who achieved enlightenment by drinking an estimated 50,000 cups of coffee), to Algernon Blackwood, an early TV celebrity who wrote the original *Starlight Express*, and Aleister Crowley – aka the Great Beast 666."

*Christopher Hirst in The Independent*

"Lachman comes into his own in his description of Charles Baudelaire and Arthur Rimbaud's flirtation with black magic."

*Rich Jevans in The Leeds Guide*

"From the Enlightenment to Modernism, ideas of the occult have shadowed literary culture, and Lachman's generous primer introduces the main exponents of diverse traditions alongside their more respectable contemporaries. The material on characters like Le Comte de St Germain and PD Ouspensky is much more interesting than the sketches of Goethe and Balzac. Nonetheless, there are sufficient curiosities to offset the occasional overstatement."

*SB Kelly in Scotland on Sunday*

"it's a sure thing that anyone with a taste for literary esoterica and magical history will learn something from *A Dark Muse*. It's a cavernous grotto full of dark glittering jewels, but one haunted by the shades of so many intriguing characters that keeping to the true path is difficult, and you lose your way forever. Verdict – Fine encyclopaedia of occult lives and thought. 9/10"

*Mark Pilkington in Fortean Times*

£9.99 ISBN 1 903517 20 6 400p B. Format

**Emperors of Dreams: Drugs in the 19th c – Mike Jay**

"Intelligent, witty, cogent and a bit pissed off, *Emperors of Dreams* is one of the best books on drugs I have come across, and should be mandatory reading for anyone concerned with drug legalisation."

*Julian Keeling in The New Statesman and Society*

"The changing status of the coca leaf is one of the many stories told by Mike Jay in his engaging survey of drug use in the 19th century. Fear of pleasure, as Jay shows in this splendid book, is perhaps the most powerful motive in the hysterical anti-drug rhetoric that has created the mess we are in today."

*Joan Smith in The Independent on Sunday*

"An excellent book . . . it states with precision as well as poetry the nature of the drug experience."

*Pick of the Week by Nicholas Lezard in The Guardian*

"Mike Jay has built a necessary bridge between scholarship and the illicit enthusiasm of drug culture . . . He does not disdain conventional drug history, but has absorbed it into a work that is literary in the broadest sense – rich in sociology and politics as well as in poetry and letters . . . Jay relishes his storytelling, and keeps a steady hand on his source material. *Emperors of Dreams* is a book for aficionados, who savour not only good writing but also the recollection, in tranquility, of altered states."

*Marek Kohn in The Independent*

"It is a fascinating book . . . Jay is excellent is on the emergence of medical science as a social force.'

*W. N. Herbert in Scotland on Sunday*

"As well as exploding the fantasy that a society without drugs used to exist, Jay clarifies the question of why so many of them were outlawed . . . in the process, he tells a series of fascinating stories about the first individuals to describe their effects, and how their use spread."

*Peter Carty in Time Out*

£9.99 ISBN 1 873982 48 8 277p B. Format

**The Dedalus Book of Decadence (Moral Ruins) – Brian Stableford**

"an invaluable sampler of spleen, everything from Baudelaire and Rimbaud to Dowson and Flecker. Let's hear it for 'luxe, calme et volupté'."

*Anne Billson in Time Out*

"*The Dedalus Book of Decadence* looks south to sample the essence of fine French decadent writing. It succeeds in delivering a range of writers either searching vigorously for the thrill of a healthy crime or lamenting their impuissance from a sickly stupor."

*Andrew St George in The Independent*

£7.99 ISBN 1 873982 01 1 210p B.Format

**The Dedalus Book of German Decadence – Ray Furness**

Decadence has been described as :'the search for the ultimate frisson, a flirtation with cruelty, a sterile and perverse sexuality, an exhausted and passive sense of dissolution and a degenerate satanism'. *The Dedalus Book of German Decadence* shows that the German contribution to this European phenomenon rivals, and frequently exceeds, the French masters. The wayward and degenerate talent of Martens, Holitscher, Przybyszewski and Ewers were matched in Austria by Sacher-Masoch and the habitués of the coffee houses (so well portrayed by Hermann Bahr), and in Prague by Paul Leppin and other young writers.

£9.99 1 873982 21 6 289p B.Format

**The Dedalus Book of Roman Decadence – Geoffrey Farrington**

"concentrates on the outrageous behaviour of the ruling class of the Roman Empire, as described in passages selected from the prose, poetry and history of the period. Their murder plots, sexual deviances, orgies, cruelty and incessant intrigue put our politicians and their peccadillos on a play school level."

*Time Out*

"devoted to the juicier bits of Tacitus, Suetonius, Juvenal, Apuleius and Seneca (the stuff that, as Gibbon put it, should be veiled in the decent obscurity of an ancient language). But you have to admit it's fun."

*Nicholas Lezard in The Guardian*

"Roman decadence is perennially mesmerising, and this book gives ample opportunity to join Tiberius, Caligula and Nero at one of their exhausting orgies. As these all involved lust and love for beautiful youths, it provides perfect bedtime reading. But what excellent reporters those Romans were – Suetonius, Tacitus, Seneca and Petronius all wrote simply and vividly and these new translations increase the immediacy."

*Gay Times*

£8.99 ISBN 1 873982 16 X 243p B.Format

**Torture Garden – Octave Mirbeau**

Oscar Wilde recommended Torture Garden to Frank Harris, describing it as 'revolting . . . a sort of grey adder.'

"First published in 1898 this decadent classic flays civilised society down to its hypocritical bones and is *le dernier cri* in kinky exoticism."

*Anne Billson in Time Out*

"A century after its first publication, this book is still capable of shocking. The opening satire is probably meaningful only to scholars of French political history, but the subsequent journey into the Far East accentuates connections between love and death, sex and depravity, fastidiousness and pleasure. And the petty, parochial corruptions of the narrator are put into context by the immersion into the Sadeian world of the Torture Garden."

*The Times*

"This hideously decadent *fin de siècle* novel by the French anarchist Mirbeau has become an underground classic. A cynical first half exposes the rottenness of politics, commerce and the petit bourgeois; in the second half, our totally corrupt narrator travels to China and meets the extraordinary Clara. She shows him the Torture Garden, a place of exotic flowers and baroque sadism. There are satirical and allegorical dimensions, but it remains irreducibly horrible."

*Phil Baker in The Sunday Times*

£7.99 ISBN 1 873982 53 4 206p B.Format

**The Episodes of Vathek – William Beckford**

"The walls of this place of terror were hidden by huge piles of carpets of a thousand kinds and a thousand hues, and these moved slowly to and fro, as if painfully stirred by human creatures stifling beneath their weight. All around were ranged black chests, whose steel padlocks seemed encrusted with blood."

Written as a continuation of *Vathek*, these are tales told in Hell by perverted individuals doomed to an eternity of suffering. They treat of such themes as necrophilia, transvestism, incest, unlimited lust and the arbitrary use of power. *The Episodes of Vathek* is a cry of despair from a man committed to a forbidden love.

£6.99 ISBN 1 873982 61 5 207p B.Format

**Là-Bas – J.K. Huysmans**

"Huysmans' dark masterpiece is a serious, uncompromisingly learned depiction of Hell through which the search for spiritual meaning must lead. The protagonist, Durtal, is investigating the life of Gilles de Rais, mass-murderer and unlikely – or not so unlikely – companion-in-arms of Joan of Arc. Long meditation on the nature of art, guilt, the satanic and the divine take him to a black mass. This superb new translation by Brendan King vividly recalls the allusive, proto-expressionist vigour of the original; images snarl and spring at the reader."

*Murrough O'Brien in The Independent on Sunday* ****

"As with most of Huysmans' books, the pleasure in reading is not necessarily from its overarching plot-line, but in set pieces, such as the extraordinary sequences in which Gilles de Rais wanders through a wood that suddenly metamorphoses into a series of copulating organic forms, the justly famous word-painting of Matthias Grunewald's Crucifixion altar-piece, or the brutally erotic scenes, crackling with sexual tension, between Durtal and Madame Chantelouve. If it is about anything, *Là*-Bas is about Good and Evil. This enlightening new translation will be especially useful to students of literature. Not only does it contain an introduction that puts Huysmans in context for those who are new to his work, it also includes extensive notes to unlock the mass of obscure words that litter the text, and references to a vast array of scientists, false messiahs and misfits whose ideas went into the concoction of this strangely fascinating book."

*Beryl Bainbridge in The Spectator*

"Sex, satanism and alchemy are the themes of this cult curio, which understandably caused shock waves in the Parisian literary world when it was first published in 1891.Its anti-hero Durtal, is researching a book on the 15th-century child murderer Gilles de Rais.Soon enough, his studies lead him to all sorts of unspeakable deeds and occults rituals. This Gothic shocker is not for the faint-hearted."

*Jerome Boyd Maunsell in The Times*

£7.99 ISBN 1 873982 74 7 304p B.Format

**The Decadent Cookbook –**
**Medlar Lucan & Durian Gray**

*Book of the year choice for Nigella Lawson in The Times & John Bayley in The Standard.*

"The chapter headings say it all: Corruption and Decay; Blood, the Vital Ingredient; The Gastronomic Mausoleum; and I Can Recommend the Poodle. This is a not a normal cookbook but a slightly sinister and highly literate feast of decadent writing on food. There are dishes from the tables of Caligula and the Marquis de Sade, a visit to Paris under siege (when rat was a luxury), some unexpected uses for cat food and some amblongous recipes from Edward Lear. There should be something here to delight and offend everyone: the recipes for cooking with endangered species looking particularly tasty. Mouthwatering."

*Phil Baker in The Sunday Times*

"Lucan and Gray, whose fruity monikers may strike some as being suspiciously apt, have concocted a fabulous and shocking assemblage."

*Christopher Hirst in The Independent*

"Arresting, too, is *The Decadent Cookbook* (including a recipe for cat in tomato sauce).

*Nigella Lawson in The Times Books of the Year*

"The putative authors are Medlar Lucan and Durian Gray, a bit of a tip-off: the medlar is a small, brown fruit, eaten when decayed; the durian fruit tastes goods but smells like sewage. These two coves left editors Alex Martin and Jerome Fletcher to tidy up this compendium of hideous repasts, taboo-busting banquets, and surprisingly sensible fare, accompanied by passages from decadent literature: menus courtesy of the Marquis de Sade, J.K.Huysmans, King George IV, the Grand Inquisitor and other gluttons."

*The Independent on Sunday*

"Not just fun but useful, containing workable recipes for Panda Paw Casserole, Cat in Tomato Sauce, and Dog à la Beti ("prior to being killed, the dog should be tied to a post for a day and hit with smallsticks, to shift the fat in the adipose tissue"), myriad blood sausages recipes, a recipe for aye-aye, of which some 20 remain in the wild, and stories by Louis de Bernieres, Huysmans, inevitably, and Charles Lamb on sucking pig. Not as you will have gathered, for the squeamish."

*Nicholas Lezard in The Guardian*

£9.99 ISBN 1 873982 22 4 224p B.Format